KILLER DEMONS

THERE IS A DEMON BEHIND EVERY PERSON!

BY

THOMA (Samuel John Naligala)

ISBN 978-93-5438-448-6

© THOMA (Samuel John Naligala) 2020

Published in India 2020 by Pencil

A brand of

One Point Six Technologies Pvt. Ltd.

123, Building J2, Shram Seva Premises,

Wadala Truck Terminal, Wadala (E)

Mumbai 400037, Maharashtra, INDIA

E connect@thepencilapp.com

W www.thepencilapp.com

DISCLAIMER: *The opinions expressed in this book are those of the authors and do not purport to reflect the views of the Publisher.*

Author biography

THOMA (Samuel John Naligala) is a capable storyteller, studied at:

A.N University, India; Fowey Lodge Bible School, and at Daybreak Film School, New Zealand. He examined film/TV shooting with Dale G. Bradley, New Zealand. He taught ESL, math, drama, film studies and Psychology at some international schools in Maldives, China, Thailand, Indonesia, Singapore and Hong Kong. At present, he retired from teaching and living in Hyderabad, India, and he gained some inputs from James Cameron (The director of Avatar).

Contents

JuvenileJack

The haziness! The white smoke rose abruptly. A white pony was running and grunting...

There was a man running for his life! The man's appearance is dull and his face isn't noticeable. There was another solid man pursuing the principal individual; the second man held the primary man and beats him to death.

The street neighs and runs quick over! Oops! Someone was dreaming!

JACK got up suddenly and glanced around; he took a look at the clock furthermore, checked the time. It was 3:45 AM. He got out of bed and left his room. He looked at his mother who was resting in the love seat while he was approaching the toilet over. There was a Holy Bible left opened on a stool at the couch. The sound of water flush came from the toilet.

Jack came out and looked at his mother; looked at the Bible; he approached the stool. He took the Bible into his hands and looked at the verse where Ruth highlighted. The verse read: "I the Lord your God am a jealous God, visiting the iniquity of the fathers on the children to the third and fourth generations of those who hate me."

Jack got mad after reading this. "I don't believe this! My eyes are really blue! How could I possibly be responsible for my ancestors' sins? How can He punish me for their sins?"

Jack spoke softly but with a disgusting tone. He banged the Bible on the floor in anger. Ruth got up suddenly! She looked at Jack who is looking at the Bible.

She got up and picked up the Bible! Holding it tight on her chest approached Jack.

"What happened, Jack? Why are you so angry and frustrated?" Ruth questioned him.

"The Bible says God will punish me because of my father's sins. It's not fair!" Jack had a valid point.

"Human reasoning falls far below the wisdom of God." Ruth explained.

"But, how could he punish me for I've not done anything immoral and unforgivable myself!" Jack was not satisfied with her answer.

"Blessings and curses are inherited! Moreover, God says things that sound strange, but however they are valid forever!" Ruth strongly believed in Almighty God.

"You know mother, I don't believe this! I never…" Lost his train of thought! He moved around restlessly. "I disagree! This is a book!"

I don't think there is another flawless book printed in the world like this one." Ruth said.

Jack came close to Ruth and looked into her eyes seriously. "I don't care! And I'm not responsible for my parents, grandparents, and great grandparents' troubles and transgressions."

Ruth could not see into the eyes of Jack. She closed her eyes.

Jack looked at her disappointedly for a couple of seconds and left immediately grabbing his jacket and wearing it.

"Heavenly father, please forgive us for we don't know your laws and principles." Ruth prayed.

***

It was early in the morning! The Screaming woods was an awesome location, they even did nights where you can brave it out in a tent. It was definitely worth a shot. If one didn't believe in ghosts then they can stay a night there and see what is exactly happening…

Jack was walking for a while... He started jogging in the woods...

Suddenly he stopped running and looked up at something hanging from a tall tree. Unbelievable! Jack was surprised to see the ghost of a schoolmaster who committed suicide there by hanging himself from a nearby tree. He did this just after World War II had ended. The children actually found him hanging on their way to school. He was seen today, hanging from that same tree dressed in a frock coat and striped trousers and a smiling mask. His name was Porter.

"I can't believe this!" Jack thought it was an illusion and when he was about to start jogging, the hanging teacher began to speak. Jack stopped and looked up.

"Howdy, Jack? Don't you bloody have a minute to say hello to me."

"Jack? How do you know me?" Jack was perplexed.

"I know everyone who lives in Pluckley village." Porter replied.

"Good for you. May I ask what you have been doing here hanging the entire night?" Jack was not afraid to speak with the ghost.

"The entire night" Porter laughed loudly, and coughed awkwardly. "You are unaware of this kid. I have been here since 1942..."

"1942? Still you are here? And alive…Sorry old man…I can't believe your story." Jack wanted to keep running.

"Many people don't believe facts; they live in fantasies all their lives." Porter looked at Jack keenly.

"Oh! Okay, man. You've got my attention. Just tell me your story briefly. And could you come down here please? I can't look up at you for too long because my neck hurts." Jack recalled what his mother said that morning.

"Okay, no worries. I can come down." Porter came down and they began walking .

When the Sub was abut rise, birds were chirping in the woods. A clod breze blown across them.

"I died just after World War II. I hung myself here. I became a ghost and I have been hanging here since then…" Porter told his story seriously.

"Unbelievable! How could this be possible? Many people died here in Pluckley...I can't see them all." Suddenly Jack calmed down, bent his head, and looked seriously while thinking. "My dad died when I was 7 years old. I can't find him anywhere around here."

"Many people die in peace... But some die and become ghosts. Demons and ghosts hang around their favorite places." Porter was trying to convince Jack.

"Is that a fact? Where do they hang around usually?" Jack was curious about the whole scenario.

"Trees, wells, by the lakes, rivers, old houses, forests, valleys, and lately they are all enjoying the views of highways, carnivals, and crowded places." Porter was talking about demons/ghosts.

"You died a long time ago. But can you actually see me?" Jack was clarifying doubts as he always wanted to know new ideas and explore unbelievable matters.

"I'm dead physically, but my spirit will never die; I can see you, follow you, trouble you, or help you." Porter spoke softly looking at Jack carefully moving his head towards Jack.

"Interesting, are you gonna trouble me? By the way, may I ask, why're you wearing a mask?" Jack whispered.

"Of course not, I see your future! I can't tell you now! I will help you understand things. I was a teacher you know! My name is POTTER, I am wearing mask to cover my age."

"Well, thank you Mr. Porter. I need to go and meet up with my friends now." Jack began jogging.

"Okay Jack! Go ahead!" Porter stood up. "See you soon!" Jack continued his jogging.

Porter went up into his hanging position; he was looking at Jack jogging...

***

A glacial lake, which lied in long ribbons among its fells, moors, and green valley in this area, which measures only about 48 to 64 kilometers. The lake was located down the highest mountain in England.

A lady named Faith is waiting there. She saw Jack approaching and smiled. Jack stopped breathing heavily and smiled.

Faith took a cigaweed from her pocket and lit it, smoked it, and handed it to Jack; Jack grabbed the cigaweed from her hand and inhaled.

"Good morning! Did you sleep well last night?" Jack asked.

"Not really! Did you eat supper last night?" Faith enquired.

"Not much. I just grabbed a bite. A hot-dog." Jack inhaled another puff and handed the cigaweed to Faith.

Faith grabbed it, inhaled it for few more seconds than before. She became serious immediately and started speaking. "In case you don't know this, I have a problem with my step-dad."

"What is the real problem here my dear?" Jack was so concerned about her.

"It's okay. Let's forget about this. I don't want to get you involved in my troubling circumstance." Faith did not want to speak about her problem, but there was no one to share her pain.

"Hey…Come on! You should share your problems with me. I can help you." Jack was suspicious.

"Yes…I need help. But, do not tell anyone! Not yet!" Faith was really afraid to reveal her problem.

"Okay, I won't." Jack assured her.

"I can't see my mother suffering from pneumonia: She is in a horrible condition with chest pain, consistent coughs and confusion, and is losing her mental awareness. And she also has a fever, sweating and shaking chills, has nausea, and shortness of breath. She is dying Jack!" Faith wept.

Jack came bit close to her and said. "I saw her in the dispensary a couple days ago. She looked pale! But what is the problem with your step-dad?"

"He is a prick! Wants me to be incest; looks at me greedily every night." The eyes of faith became red.

"Bastard… How dare he?" Jack looked into the eyes of her and understood how she was suffering.

"But he's taking care of my mother. I can't fight with him; and please don't get involved in this." Faith was good friend of Jack, and she always was caring him.

"Why should I stay away from this? Do you see how bad the situation is already?" Jack wanted solve her problem.

"Please do not cause any more problems for me. I know how to handle this problem on my own." She looked at across and saw a man was coming towards them. John was jogging and approaching them.

"See, here comes; your problem!" Faith spoke softly. "My problem…" Jack got confused.

"Yes, indeed! John wanted me, but he couldn't maintain a commitment for that."

As she finished smoking, John arrived. "Hi John" Jack wished.

John and Jack show their fists! Faith took another cigaweed from her pocket, lit it and began smoking quickly.

John smiled at Jack and looked at Faith "Hi, Jack, Hi Faith, How long have you guys been here for?"

"Just now…" Faith replied.

"How's your fitness training going on John?" Jack questioned John, taking the cigaweed from Faith.

"It's working out very well for me and I am soon going to have a six-pack." John was confident.

"Good for you! Have you got anything to do today?" Jack inhaled the smoke.

"Yes, got something for you." John took a small bottle of rum and handed it to Jack.

"Thanks!" Jack took it; opened the lid and drank it quickly.

Jack gulped the rum and felt great. Faith looked reluctantly at both Jack and John.

"You see, I have of plenty of these" John mentioned about alcohol. "I have been thinking…and got some ideas…We could go ahead and organize fights. We could earn money."

"It's illegal John." Faith said seriously.

"Legal rules are made by us. We can break them if needed." Jack replied and looked at her.

"Jack…it's a dangerous sport." Faith was concerned about Jack.

"Dangerous! But we're not afraid. We're going to do it anyway." John declared.

"Yes, we will do it anyway." Jack agreed.

"Okay…I will be the cheer girl!" As she always wanted to be with Jack, Faith agreed to Jack.

Jack turned back and looked into the woods. "Did you notice that?" Jack questioned. "What?" John asked curiously.

"Someone is watching us!" Jack expressed a doubt. "You have OCD Jack." Faith spoke softly.

"Yes, I know." Jack still focused on woods. "I do not see anyone there Jack." John stated.

"Never mind... You're right. No one is there. Shall we have a bet?" Jack asked John.

"You guys started again with betting?" Faith was sarcastic about their addition.

"Why not…ten bucks each" John said.

They both handed over ten bucks each to Faith.

"Wait…I need to go home." Faith did not want to stay.

"Hold on. Be back in a couple of minutes." Jack and John told her and began their race.

While they were running around the lake, Faith looked at them reluctantly. They both ran fast equally. But Jack won the race. They returned to Faith, breathing heavily.

"You know…betting is illegal and addictive." Faith told them.

"But racing is thrilling!" Jack did not want to take any advice from her.

"Yes, we all race in our lives." John wanted to convince Faith.

"I agree, you need to strive to achieve what you truly desire. But in acceptable ways only." Faith was so firm and practical about life skills.

***

There was a catholic church in the Pluckley village. Jack's mother Ruth was sweeping in front of the Church. Jack approached her.

"Jack…my son, where have you been the entire morning?" Ruth looked at him affectionately.

"I jogged and spent some time with my friends." Jack answered.

"Christmas is approaching. Could you do me a favor?" She requested him.

"What is it mother?" Jack looked at the tower of the church.

"Could you please help the youth with decorating the church?"

"I will mother. But not today, tomorrow, okay? Jack had some plans for the day.

"Okay, my son – God bless you." Ruth was happy for he agreed to help.

When Jack was about to leave, Ruth said. "Hold on! Our bishop Rev. Joseph wants to have a word with you."

Jack was bit hesitant to see the pastor.

"You can find him in the church office, over there..." Ruth pointed towards the church office.

"Now…mother?" Jack did not want to go. Ruth nodded yes, and then Jack walked towards the church office.

***

Pastor Steve was sitting in his chair and making sermon notes from the Holy Bible. Jack knocked on the door.

"Come in" Steve said, and Jack entered. "Good morning pastor" Jack wished him. "Good morning son, please come and take your seat" Steve smiled. Jack said, "Thanks" and sat in a chair across Steve's table.

"Jack, I just want to re-confirm with you that the love of Jesus Christ is constant." Steve meant that Christ loves Jack.

"I appreciate that. My mother tells me the same every day." Jack did not have a strong faith in what Stave said.

"Yes, Ruth is so kind and humble. She loves you very much." Steve acknowledged mother's love.

"She does her best." Jack was not interested in this conversation

"Jack, I request you to help with the arrangements for the upcoming Christmas celebration."

"I will do my best." Jack replied and wanted to leave.

"Before you leave, I just want to tell you that God is very powerful and that we can't argue with Him about His wisdom which is comparatively so high above human understanding and reasoning." Steve wanted to counsel Jack.

Jack was clicking his shoes and looking around.

Mary, daughter of Steve Joseph entered through the backdoor with a tray and tea kettle.

"Good morning father. Good morning Jack." "Bless you my daughter!"

"Good morning Mary!" Jack wished her. Mary smiles at Jack and served a cup of tea to him and her dad. Jack took the cup, and said "Thank you Mary!"

"Jack, if you have time would you please join us in performing in the musical." Mary asked Jack.

"I have no interest in music." Jack replied seriously.

"Jack is going to help us decorate the Church." Steve looked at Jack.

"Oh! Okay…" Mary smiled at Jack.

Jack finished drinking the tea and handed over the cup to Mary.

"Thank you Mary! The tea is tasty. Thank you Pastor." Jack stood up.

"God bless you Jack!" Steve stood up and shook hands with Jack.

"See you tomorrow Jack!" Mary was happy to see Jack.

"So long…" Jack left the room while Mary was looking at him admiringly.

***

Ruth was about finish cleaning. Jack waked away waving his hand to Ruth. "Bye mother! Today is going to be a big day!"

"Take care of yourself Jack!" Ruth waved her hand.

***

Jack was riding a bicycle with Faith on the back seat.

"How's your mother, Faith?"

"Suffering, you know it's a chronic disease." Faith felt sad.

"I'm sorry, but do not worry, things will change." Jack assured.

"She hates this village, and wants me to move somewhere else and live happily." Faith also wanted the same as she did not like to live in Pluckley village.

"I know…your step dad is a weirdo" Jack was angry and suddenly he stopped as he saw Porter just in front of him. Jack gets off the bicycle. But Faith couldn't see anything.

"What happened? Why did you stop?" Faith asked.

"Would you please take this bicycle and go to the spot. I will join you in a few minutes." Jack requested her.

"Why? What happened?" Faith got confused. "I'll explain later. Please go!" Jack insisted. "Are you alright Jack?" Faith looked worried.

Jack looks at her seriously; Faith understood and said "Okay, I'm leaving"

Faith rode the bicycle alone.

"How're you Jack?" Porter asked. I'm okay, sir." Jack answered.

"What's up? Where are you heading?" Porter looked at the way Faith went.

"Well…we are going to organize kickboxing competitions by the river." Jack answered.

"Wow! Who are you going to fight? I hope you fight and win." Porter was so excited.

"My friend John, myself, and other fighters from nearby villages…Thanks for your support" Jack felt warm.

"Great! Any spectators, and any bets?" Porter liked the sport all his life.

"Yes, there will be gathering and there will be betting too" Jack looked at the way Faith went.

"I'm excited…May I go with you? Please!" Porter requested.

"You're welcome, but are you visible?" Jack expressed a doubt.

"No worries. I will be visible to you only. Besides, you will be the only one who can hear my voice. No one else will be able to see or hear me." Porter whispered.

"Cool! Please come with me." Jack began walking. "Thank you Jack…" Porter followed Jack.

As they both walked towards the riverside, Potter sings: "War, huh, yeah...What is it good for, absolutely nothing! War, huh, yeah...What is it good for, absolutely nothing! Say it again... Why 'all...'" While he was singing, Jack walked rhythmically and lit a cigaweed.

***

As the music continued, Jack and Potter approached the riverside street.

John and Faith were waiting for Jack. Approximately 70 people had gathered for the fight. Adam, the organizer made an announcement to the people who have gathered in the area.

"Hello folks!! Welcome to the JJF Kickboxing challenge!! Admission is 10 pounds at the gate, and 5 pounds if you buy your tickets a day in advance. The whole event is one huge Pluckley Village party, perfect for a fun night out with friends."

Adam started collecting entry fees while Jack and John are getting ready for the fight. Some of the men were drunk and staring at Faith. Faith lights a cigaweed.

Invisible Potter was observing the entire crowd. He approached some drunkards and they smell weird. "Bloody people... I can't bare their smell." Porter felt disgusting.

Faith approached some people and said aloud. "I bet on Jack 20 for10. He is going to win."

"How do you know that?" A man gave ten bucks to Faith.

"She might have seen his power." Another man gave ten.

"Shut up you morons. We are here to get entertained, not to entertain a lady." The third man bet on John and gave ten to Faith.

Faith blew smoke in the face of Man 3 and cheer for Jack in the crowd.

"Jack, my darling, you will win the game for me."

Jack waved at the crowd and Faith smiled. Referee Richard entered the ring.

"Jack and John are going to fight now in a few minutes; bet on one man; guess who will win.

Your man wins, and you will win double the money you bet. Come on folks, hurry…bet your money on your man. You bet on Jack go to our beautiful lady Faith and for John hand over your money to me." Porter announced loudly, and continued explaining the rules.

"Underground fighting is an illegal and dangerous activity. Sometimes people will get killed in street fights. Just being here is a crime because you are considered a supporter even if you're not fighting or betting."

Porter was so excited and looked around. The riverside was full of garbage, plastic waste, soda cans and liquor bottles. The lights overhead had barely enough wattage to see who is fighting.

Adam waved and yelled. "Let's begin the fight"

Jack was twenty-five years old. His face was scarred and thick around the nose. His black hair shined and hung in his eyes. Jack was a fighter in a plodding, machine-like style. John was reaching his thirties.

John danced and banged combinations into Jack's face with great accuracy. But the punches did not even cause Jack to blink…He grinned at his opponent and kept grinding ahead. The people were clamour for blood…They heckled the fighters. In the thick smoke they resembled spectres. Everyone is hustled bets…The action was heavier around. An old man yelled for somebody to cover a two pounds bet.

The BELL RINGS and the fighters returned to their corners. Somebody threw a beer can into the ring. John spat something red in a bucket and sneered across the ring at Jack.

A car approached the spot. Two girls got out. They approached John and teased Faith. The crowd yelled and cheered.

Adam and Faith were busy collecting betting money from the crowd. The GAMBLERS call out new odds - ten to one for Jack, the underdog.

Two cheer girls approached John and kissed him. "I'm gonna bust his head wide open!" John said.

"I expect no less John." One girl whispered. Meanwhile second girl showed her middle finger to Faith, But Faith did not care.

A man who bets on John shouted aloud. "Hey…waltz- in' -- Give the suckers some action."

"Hey…" Jack waved his right hand to his supporters in the audience.

Jack's supporters reacted and yelled. Invisible Potter approached Jack and said, "You're moving like a bum. Want some advice?"

"No sir! Let me do this myself!" Jack replied.

 Jack looked at Faith and she was looking at him strangely and spoke to herself, "With whom he is talking?"

"Never mind, you can see what I can." Jack told her aloud.

The BELL Rang…Jack made the sign of the cross. The fighters engaged in battle. John clinched Jack and purposely butted him. The butt opened a bleeding cut on the corner of Jack's eye.

Jack became furious over the foul and drove a flurry of punches into John's body. Jack slammed John in the jaw and John was knocked out for now. The fans threw rubbish into the ring. Jack ignored it. The fans loudly went about collecting bets. The referee didn't bother to even count John out and dragged him under the ropes to hand him over to his girls.

A new fighter named Bob entered the ring. Jack slipped on a tattered robe. Embroidered clumsily on the back was, "The Lion."

"Winner, Jack Reid -- Next fighter is the Bulldozer Bob from Edinburgh." Referee announced.

Faith kissed Jack.

The two girls helped John walk towards their car. Jack watched for a moment and continued to prepare for the next round.

Potter approached Jack, and said, "Congratulations…Jack, I thought it would take a long time to finish the fight, but you knocked John out in a couple of minutes! Great work!"

"Thanks Potter." Jack waved at the crowd.

"You're very welcome Jack…Now let me go and see what's happening with the crowd." Potter moved around.

"Okay…enjoy! My invisible friend..." Jack replied.

Potter moved around the crowd carefully as he could see people and they couldn't see him, but something happened… Potter saw someone…a woman wearing a modern gown that is derived from the robe worn under the cappa clausa, a garment resembling a long black cape. Her dress was traditionally made of black cloth, and the material at the back of the gown was gathered into a yoke. Her gown had bell-shaped sleeves. She looked at Potter and ignored him.

"Who're you? May I ask what you are doing here?" Potter approached her.

"I'm Clara. I live in the vicinity." Clara replied.

"How can you see me…I mean how could I possibly see you and speak with you?" Potter was perplexed.

"What do you think of yourself?" Clara whispered.

"I'm an invisible ghost from the forest; and I was a schoolteacher." Potter whispered.

"Well…I was a school principal." Clara spoke proudly.

"School Principal…Well…alright, but are you from one among the ghosts from a school that burnt out a long time ago?" Potter questioned.

"Yes…you know something? I burnt down the school myself." Clara clarified.

"May I ask why did you do that? Potter was curious.

"I fell in love with a student. And they said I'm unfit as a principal. I got so angry that I decided to burn the school down." Clara felt sad and vengeful.

"Interesting…May I know, why are you here now?" Potter wanted to know more details.

"I am with a young man and I love him." Clara stared at the crowd.

"Is he your student then…alive now…" Potter got confused.

"No…no…no…he is a great grandson of my student lover then." Clara cleared his doubt.

"Very interesting, do you speak with him?" Potter was surprised to see another ghost in the vicinity.

"No…I just follow him, guide him, and protect him." Clara felt reluctance and looked seriously at Potter and said, "A principal like me can't chat with a teacher any longer than this. You are discharged!

Potter got baffled and said "Yes…Madam Clara…Thank you for your time."

Clara looked at her young man and approached him and stood behind him. The young man felt a cold breeze touched his ears.

Potter strained his eyes to see a CAMERAMAN entered the area with a light man. Adam announced, "Now, I have a special announcement for everyone here tonight. For the first time in many years, this championship fight is gonna be on the WhatsApp. It is free for the visitors; if you want see the fight on your mobiles, please give me your WhatsApp numbers before you leave."

 Silence loomed over the area…Bob was apprehensive. The scene was becoming too real. The frightened cameraman and his assistant were getting ready to shoot the fight.

Bob suddenly stepped forward and hit Jack very hard across the side of the head…The place became stone cold. Bob was in total command and enjoying every moment of the fight. The GAMBLERS call out new odds - one to ten for Bob, the tough fighter.

"What's happening here?" Referee asked Bob.

"I'm happening! This pig is no match for me. I am a contender. He's nothing." Bob replied proudly.

"Well…Bob, this is a match. You need to win and show your power, but not before…" Referee warned Bob.

"Don't disrespect me old man. I'll knock you out too. C'mon wop, spar me, let everybody see who's got the heat around here." Bob threatened the match referee.

John recovered and came out of his car along with his girls. Bob looked at John and smirked. Bob turns to Jack and made donkey sounds. "If you're afraid to fight me then get down here and kiss my feet boy."

Faith looked nervously around and knew it's only seconds before the blood will run. Jack stood still, closed his eyes for a while, thought of a plan – how to knockout this giant Bob.

Faith ran to Jack and said, "Jack…Please, don't take a chance. He wants to hurt you so you can't fight."

Jack swallowed his pride. He still had the string around his ankles. He started to shuffle away with Faith…Bob st ep forward and viciously slapped Jack again.

This time the crowd yelled and enjoyed the act. They were all entertaining and gone mad.

Referee was so serious about Bob's action, "Why are you ignoring the rules man! Back off scumbag or I'll bite your face off!"

Bob cut loose with a hook and knocked the Referee flat. The crowd freaked of fear…Faith's eyes flicked back and forth between Jack and Bob. Immediately,

Adam fired the fire ring; the flames rose…

"Now boy, kiss my feet." Bob was coming close to Jack.

Jack looked at the referee lying on the floor. He shuffled forward and stood before Bob.

Bob pointed at his feet and ordered Jack almost in a whisper, "…Kiss 'em."

Jack looked at the Referee again and then lowered his eyes to Bob's feet. Bob smiled. Jack started to bend towards Bob's shoes. Without warning, he exploded with a pair of combinations into Bob's exposed ribs.

A CRACK is HEARD and Bob sank to the floor writhing in pain. The place was silent except for Bob's moaning. The fire entered Bob's eyes. He could not see! Faith was stunned by the scene. The place became a very gloomy place. Potter eyes Jack with admiration and a hint of apprehension…and then he looked at Bob.

"Oh…My…God, I can't see anything; my eyes are gone!" Potter approached Bob and whispered in his ears. "I'm sorry man…this is misery! I don't think you will ever recover and fight again. I thought you understood that those who boast about themselves will be down-founded soon enough." But Bob could not hear Potter.

Faith was the first one to shake off the chill. She shook her fists at the crowd and puts her arm around Jack and said aloud, "My man here has cannons--remember that."

The crowd was disappointed over Bob's knockout; dispersed, leaving Bob lying on the dirty ground. Some men looked back at a pathetic and broken figure of Bob.

Jack and Faith along with Adam came forward to help Bob to stand up. And Jack gave him an energy drink, while Faith did first-aid to Bob.

John and his girls approached them; Jack looked at them and requested, "John, could you please take this guy to his village or any nearby hospital in your car?" John Nodded 'yes'; looked at Adam and said, "Okay…Jack, well done today!"

Adam looked at John and said, "We've got money! We will sit and share our profits tomorrow."

Jack helped Bob reach the car and board it. John and his girls along with injured Bob left.

Adam left in his motorbike. Jack and Faith left the place in their bicycle.

***

Christ's Birthday

It was Christmas Eve; Santa Claus was standing at the gate of the church, who was a portly, joyous, white- bearded man with spectacles, wearing a red coat with a white fur collar and cuffs, white-fur-cuffed red trousers, a red hat with white fur, and a black leather belt and boots. Also, he carried a bag full of gifts for the children.

Santa was ringing a bell and speaking loudly.

"Merry Christmas everyone, gifts for the good children; come and collect…Adults…Come and donate pence for the children's gifts."

Children approached Santa with joy and happiness. Santa distributed some gifts and chocolates to all of the children. Meanwhile Jack approached Santa and said, "Hey, Santa… from the East. You bring the American culture here."

"Santa is universal; you can find him all over the world." Santa replied. "Universal…yeah…From Babylon to Britain…" Jack was sarcastic.

"Babylon?" Santa was confused and didn't understand

"You won't understand…Santa" Jack tried to pull off Santa's beard, but Santa escaped.

"I'm out of here!" Jack went into the Church.

***

The church was decorated with colorful clothes and florescent papers. Ruth welcomed Jack. Mary Jones and members of the church youth and children were practicing a skit called "The Nativity Story." And some of the youth and children were decorating the Church.

"Jack, good to see you here…" Ruth was happy to see her son.

"Mother, how beautiful this season is? Tomorrow is Christmas!" Jack looked around and looked at Mary who was keenly looking at him.

"Yes, indeed…the season of joy and prosperity…" Ruth said joyfully.

"Celebrating the birth of Christ the messiah…" Jack felt warm and hugged his mother.

Meanwhile Mary approached Jack and Ruth and wished Jack, "Merry Christmas Jack…"

"Merry Christmas Mary…" Jack shook hands with Mary.

"Would you like to help with the decoration or would you like to act in the skit? We could use your help either way." Mary asked Jack.

"Sorry…I'm not a very good actor." Jack replied.

"How about guiding those decorators?" Mary requested.

"Will do…" Jack looked at Ruth.

"Thank you very much…" Mary was glad.

"My pleasure…" Jack was looking at Mary admiringly.

"If you will excuse me, I'm going to go see Pastor Joseph in his office." Ruth wanted to go, but Jack held her hand and said, "Mother…A small request."

"What is it my dear?" Ruth asked.

"I would like to address the congregation tomorrow…Just for ten minutes. Would you ask Pastor's permission?" Jack stood next to Mary and asked.

"Very well…I will seek permission." Ruth left to pastor's office.

"Interesting…perhaps, you could speak on behalf of the church youth." Mary suggested.

"I will if given a chance." Jack replied.

"It's our tradition. On Christmas Eve, one young person and one elder speak after the ceremony."

Mary wanted to encourage Jack. She have had a soft corner towards Jack and always liked his company.

Jack felt happy and said, "I will go and help with the decorations."

"Thank you Jack…" Mary patted him on the shoulder.

Jack went to the decorating youth, and Mary followed Jack. Jack looked at the actors' group practicing the skit. They were all singing a popular song "Silent night…Holy night."

***

Jack was asleep that night. He had recurring nightmares of a white stallion; he saw a man of unknown identity with a white horse on his charm bracelet. The trails of tainted moonshine lead back to the murderer. Upon finally cornering the crook on Christmas, fireworks busted overhead, Jack tried to see the face of the person who murdered his father, 20 years ago, on the same night. There was only one clue - The murderer could be recognizable by the white stallion on his bracelet.

Jack was struggling…he couldn't see the face of the murderer. He was experiencing a nightmare in an archaic sense which consisted of being paralyzed except for his eyes, feeling a heavy weight on his chest and being unable to call out for help.

He really was undergoing strong feelings of terror. He saw a cruel face of a king, wearing a mask, but surprisingly the king is actually wearing the exact same outfit of Santa; he shouted at his servants and orders them to decorate a huge tree; that tree looked like the Christmas tree; and Jack assisted with decorating but it had unexpected details which displayed it as a monochromatic Christmas tree.

They were hanging the tree topper from the ceiling; with special ornaments, round paper lantern mirrors the round ornaments on the tree. They were attaching a ceiling hook right above the tree's tallest point enable the lantern to float by hanging it from a bow attached to the hook. For added impact, they were attaching cascading ribbon or garland from the bottom of the hanging tree topper. This modern

Christmas tree decoration made a big impact without appearing over-decorated or tired, and it stood out among the rest in creativity and originality.

Jack woke up suddenly; he exited his room and went to the toilet. Ruth was sleeping on the couch as usual. Jack flushed the toilet and came out to see his mother. He wanted to speak about his nightmare. He looked at The Holy Bible opened and kept on the stool near the couch. Ruth was asleep.

Jack looked at the Bible; took the Bible into his hands and started reading: Isaiah 53:1-3

"Who has believed what we have heard? And to whom has the arm of the Lord been revealed? He was despised and rejected by others; a man of suffering and acquainted with infirmity; and as one from whom others hid their faces he was despised and we held him on no account."

Ruth got up and looked at Jack.

"Jack, my son" She looked at the Bible in his hands, "Are you ok?"

"Okay…Mother! I had a nightmare!"

"God will keep us safe…only if we read the scriptures and pray!"

"Never mind," He placed the Bible back on the stool. "I'm going out for a jog."

"Take care, my son." Jack left and Ruth began the Bible watch.

***

Jack was jogging fast and stopped at a place. He was breathing high, looked around and was frustrated. Potter approached him then and wished.

"Good morning Jack! How've you been?" "I'm okay…" Jack was still breathing heavily.

"You look terrified, may I ask what happened?" Potter could hear the thumping sound of Jack's heart from his chest.

"I had a nightmare!" Jack looked like a terrified child to Potter.

"What about…" Potter asked.

"I saw a shadow of the killer who killed my dad twenty years ago." Jack explained.

"I'm sorry…Jack? Any clues…" Potter felt bad.

"I always see a white stallion attached to his bracelet; I could see his hand, but his face was in the darkness." Jack was clear about his dream.

"Just one clue…I will see what I can do." Potter wanted to help Jack.

"Thank you Potter…I will if have any clue" Jack felt bit relaxed then.

"What else my dear…" Potter wanted to make Jack feel normal.

"I saw an ugly king who dressed like Santa; and some of his servants were decorating the Christmas tree for him." Jack was not afraid about this part of the dream.

"I see" Potter began thinking and recalling his memories. "December 25th was, at first, celebrated as that of the reborn, pagan God of Babylon: Tammuz. This early time of Babylon, to the rest of the ancient world and this, of course, includes ancient Rome. Just as with the holidays of Easter and Halloween, new names would be inserted for these original Gods of Babylon, according to each empire or nation which adopted it! And just like Easter and Halloween, the Christmas festival also seemed connected to the cycles of nature such as the changing of the seasons!"

"Very interesting…Jesus and his parents or disciples neither mentioned his birthday nor celebrated it." Jack had a smart mind and authentic researching skills.

"Well said. Christmas wasn't originally "Christ's day," but an amalgamation of sorts. Christian shell, which is called as pagan underbelly; and, what about some of the other famous elements of this day - such as the Christmas tree? Are they followers of Christ; or something more? Where did this come from?" Potter said seriously.

"I'm listening, Potter…" Jack expected more details.

"We see it all comes from a pagan origin. What is all of this paganism about? Could the Bible have a little something to say about the use of plants such as this in these ways? Yes, the "Christmas tree," interestingly enough, may have been among those pagan elements. Xmas Trees were an early Babylonian custom to go out and place a gift on a tree at the

Winter solstice which begins on the 25th of December as an offering to Tammuz - the Sun God." Potter clarified.

"Thank you Potter...you really are a nice teacher! I appreciated your interpretation of my dream. I now understand the truth about the Christmas festival." Jack's heart beat came to normal.

"My pleasure Jack...by the way...I wanted to tell you something." Potter gained Jack's attention.

"What is it sir?" Jack asked while they started walking in the woods.

"I saw a lady ghost the other day when you were fighting by the river." Potter was thrilled to meet the ghost of Clara and wanted to tell Jack.

"A lady ghost...Who is she?" Jack asked.

"Well...She calls herself a school principal. And she has a strange story. She's a fan of a kid who was there watching the fight." Potter couldn't believe the love story of Clara.

"Strange!" Jack was smiling.

"Yes, indeed! I need to know more about her. I will let you know later." Potter assured.

"Okay...thanks for the help!" Jack stopped and looked at Potter and tried shook hands with him in vain.

"You're very welcome Jack...I'm visible to you only." Potter couldn't shake hands with Jack.

"I need to go and see my girl. Bye teacher!" Jack realized that Faith was waiting for him.

"Bye for now…see you again later Jack!" Potter waved his hand.

Jack starts jogging and goes towards the lake, while Potter looked at Jack.

***

Jack reached the lake hurriedly and looked around for Faith. There was no sign of her. He sat on a rock and lit a cigaweed; inhaled and released smoke. When the smoke spread, Faith appeared very close to Jack's face wearing a ghost mask to try and threaten him.

Jack feared not and removes her mask with a quick reflex. Faith sat next to Jack and said,

"Oh! Come on Jack. Don't be afraid of ghosts."

"We have ghosts all around us; why should I care?" Jack clarified and shared his personal knowledge about ghosts.

"What do you mean…Do you see any ghosts behind me?" Faith was kidding, but surprised on Jack's comments.

"Yes, I can see one behind you." Jack looked behind from on her shoulders.

"Behind me…You're kidding, aren't you?" Faith looked back.

"I'm not kidding Faith…I see what I see!" Jack thought Faith was really frightened.

"Jack, you are suffering from illusions and disorders?" Faith knew about Jack was suffering from disorders.

"But I see what I see." Jack replied.

"Well, what do you see?" Faith was curious and wanted have some fun.

"I see you are bearing the pain at home. I see you are being tormented by wicked people." Jack was so concerned about her emotional distress.

Faith looked at Jack and after a few seconds tears came out of her eyes and crawled down her cheeks.

"You're right Jack. I couldn't face my step-dad. He's an evil person."

"I'm so desperate. I dropped out of college…couldn't find a job. I'm a loser…I'm a loser." Jack wanted to help by taking care of Faith and her mother; leaving this ghost village to another safe place.

"Don't worry Jack…God says that he won't punish people for so long and with unbearable pain." Faith had some faith in God.

"Is that a fact? I believe you Faith. You will be with me all my life." Jack assured.

"Well, I will be with you forever…But…" She became silent.

"What happened?" Jack asked.

"John is sending flowers every day and he wanted to marry me." Faith laid her head on Jack's shoulders.

"Oh…yeah…how dare he?" Jack was angry.

"I rejected his proposal. He is so angry!" Faith was comfortably relaxing on Jack's shoulders.

"I'll speak with him." Jack assured.

Faith got up and extended her hand, "Come on, Jack… let's run around the lake."

Jack held her hand and got up. They both jogged around the lake. The sun rose slowly while they were jogging.

***

Call from London

That was Christmas day. All the villagers gathered in the church. They were all happy wearing new cloths. Pastor Joseph was sharing the good news of the birth of Christ. Jack was sitting next to his mother Ruth while she held Jack's hand.

***

Behind that church there was a burial ground. There was smoke and mist all over the place. There were some shadows appearing behind the mist. There was Potter standing and there were many ghosts standing behind and besides Potter.

The ghost of Clara approaches Potter. "Hello teacher. Merry Christmas…"

Potter was perplexed and cleared his throat, "Merry Christmas Madam Clara! Good to see you again."

"Could you please move a step back? You're not supposed to stand next to the principal." Clara still believed that protocol.

"As you say Madam..." Potter stood back.

While the church was singing "Jay to the World" beautifully and the ghosts felt overwhelmed listening to that song.

"They're remixing authentic songs, aren't they Potter?" Clara expressed her doubt.

"Yes, Madam...the new generation is weird and the new tunes are noisy!" Potter agreed to her.

"No discipline at all...they're burning their bright future." Clara felt disgusting.

"Yes, Madam Clara...they are burning their lives. Do you know why these many ghosts are present here?" Potter asked.

Clara looked at him weirdly. Potter understood her feelings, and said,

"I come here for the first time Madam Clara."

"I see...they are all following their favorite individuals who attend the church today. Aren't you following any yourself?" Clara clarified.

"Yes, I have a friend." Potter answered.

"Good for you. Life is boring without friends." Clara stated.

"May I ask what you do with your boy? Do you help him pass his academic tests?" Potter wanted to more about her lover boy.

"I was the principal...but not now. I just love my boy and influence him to be a lover boy!" Clara was so proud to speak about her boy.

Potter looked around at all of the ghosts present there. He was perplexed and said, "Oh! I can guess now...all of us are influencing living persons around us. I need to go and see what's happening in the Church."

Clara said, "You may go"

Potter reached the window and is surprised to see Jack speaking.

"Merry Christmas to all of the people gathered here in the Church today. Christmas is a happy occasion! We celebrate the birth of Christ on December 25th every year. And we celebrate our birthdays every year as well. We know, when we are born, we celebrate. But nobody knows for sure that Christ was born on the 25th of December."

Deacon Samuel raised his hand asked Jack, "So what's your point?"

"December 25th was at first meant to celebrate the rebirth of the pagan God of Babylon Tammuz. This practice must have spread beyond this early time of Babylon to the rest of the ancient world, and this, of course, includes Ancient Rome. Just as with the holidays of Easter and Halloween, new names would be inserted for these original Gods of Babylon, according to each empire or nation which adopted it. And, just like Easter and Halloween, this festival also seemed connected to the cycles of nature; such as the changing of the seasons!"

Everyone looked at Jack strangely and reluctantly.

"Please finish your point and vote of thanks! We're all hungry." Deacon Samuel told Jack.

"We might think they are celebrating the true Savior, when taking part in Christmas celebrations; when they are actually continuing the celebration of some false savior - another older pagan "Jesus!" This could also help us to understand better why the apostle Paul wrote to the Corinthians: to beware of the subtle deceit of "another Jesus whom we have not preached." Last but not the least, Christmas was illegal in America until 1836 as it was considered an ancient pagan holiday." After listing to Jack everyone in the Church experienced an emotional shock.

"I thank our beloved Pastor Joseph, the Deacons, the youth, and the whole congregation and I wish you all a very Merry Christmas!" Jack concluded and returned to his seat.

The entire congregation got up and began talking to each other about Jack's statements…They were surprised, but the church elders were angry with Jack. Ruth was also shocked.

Deacon Samuel approached Ruth angrily and said, "Mrs. Ruth Reid, could you please meet us in the church office after the feast. Also, bring you son Jack with you."

"Okay…Mr. Samuel." Ruth was afraid.

Jack stood near the window observing people around in the area. All of them were looking at him with rejection and obsession. Mary approached Jack, while Potter is observing them both from outside.

"What've you done Jack?!! I pleaded my dad to give you a chance to speak." Mary was upset.

"I'm sorry Mary…I feel what I feel. I don't see happiness in the traditional practices." Jack replied.

"You disappointed me Jack. I think you're sick and are suffering from illusions and emotional disturbances." Mary was angry.

"I'm not normal …Ms. Mary. And I thank you for your help."

Faith approached Jack. Mary left angrily and disappointed. Curtis, the step-dad of Faith looked at Faith disgustingly.

Potter was calling Jack from outside the window. "Jack… Jack…" Jack looked around and noticed Potter .

"Potter…What're you doing here?" Jack was surprised to see the ghost in the campus of the church.

"I'm here for the feast in the graveyard with many ghosts." Potter answered.

"Are you kidding?" Jack couldn't believe.

"Yes, partly…feast is a lie. But I met so many of my kind in the graveyard behind the church." Potter was happy.

"Is that a fact?" Jack couldn't believe yet.

"Yes, come and see…No…no…no, you can't see them." Potter wanted to reveal the scene to Jack.

"I can see you though." Jack expressed a doubt.

"Strangely enough, I don't want that Lady to see you." Potter was taking about Clara.

"Who's that? Is that your principal?" Jack wanted to tease Potter.

"Well… FYI, she's not my principal." Potter told seriously.

"Okay…the principal" Jack was smiling.

"Yeah… a school principal…very irritating person" Potter replied.

Ruth approached Jack. She was disappointed and sad. "Son, what've you done today?"

"I spoke what I believed" Jack replied seriously.

Ruth held Jack's hand and said, "Come, let's go to the Office. They want to speak with you."

"Okay…mother, as you say so." Jack went with her. Potter wanted to say something to Ruth in vain. She couldn't hear anything.

***

Pastor Joseph, Deacons Samuel and Curtis, and some other church members are waiting for Jack. Jack and Ruth entered.

No one in the room was happy to see Jack's face; in fact they were all very angry.

***

Visible Faith and invisible Potter were waiting outside.

Potter was talking to himself. "Jack is all right! I agree with his opinions on Christ's birthday celebrations."

Faith was speaking to herself. "What the f**k is this meeting about? These so called blessed people are really able to judge Jack?"

Potter looked around and sees all of the ghosts are following their human mates, whispering in their ears. And he looked at Clara and is surprised to see how she is dealing with her boy.

"It's so unfortunate Jack! I was shocked to hear your speech." Pastor Joseph said.

"Well…With due respect…Pastor Joseph, I just expressed my views about the Christmas celebrations." Jack tried and explained.

"Who are you to criticize our traditions? What qualifications do you have?" Deacon Samuel questioned angrily.

"Qualifications…" Jack was upset.

"Son, apologize to your elders." Ruth advised.

"I do apologize mother, but only when I actually do make a mistake." Jack spoke confidently.

Pastor Joseph looked keenly at Jack.

"Jack is a juvenile delinquent in our village; he is aggressive and rude; moreover, he is friends with my daughter and other young people in our village; they are all taking intoxicating drugs and are involved in illegal secret fights." Another Deacon and the step-dad of Faith blamed Jack.

"Is that a fact? What do you say Jack?" Samuel questioned.

"I agree…Whatever Mr. Curtis said is right." Jack was just looking at Ruth and noticed tears in her eyes.

Pastor Joseph stood up from his chair and approached Ruth, turned towards Jack and said, "Well Jack, if you don't believe in our worship system I advise you to not attend the Church anymore."

"Pastor, please forgive him." Ruth broke out in tears.

"I forgive him Ruth, but his presence in the Church creates problems." Joseph expressed helplessness.

"Jack…We hereby expel you from our Church from today and onwards." Samuel declares.

"Brother Samuel…Please…" Ruth pleaded. "Sorry Mrs. Ruth! I can't help you." Samuel said.

"Mother…you need not to beg. This is my issue." Jack held hands of Ruth.

"Jack…I wish you could just leave our village because your existence here is troublesome. You are a troubled young man and have always been out of sorts. I heard you are suffering from some behavioral problems." Curtis spoke sarcastically. There is rejection and dislike in his voice.

"Brother Curtis, you can't just throw him out of the village." Pastor Joseph told boldly.

"Pastor Joseph, thank you for your advice. I won't attend your Church hereafter. Now if you will excuse me, I have to go." Jack wanted to leave the room.

"You may go, Jack! God bless you!" Pastor was concerned about Ruth and her services to the church.

Jack left the room quickly while Ruth looked at him sadly, and Curtis looked at him cruelly.

Joseph, Samuel, and Curtis were talking among each other and are looking at Ruth, who stood there helplessly.

***

Jack came out and looked at Faith and Potter seriously and said "They expelled me from the Church."

"How dare they?" Faith questioned.

"Oh! No…How rude are these Church elders? No one can judge people, except God!" Potter told his opinion.

"Well…I'm not surprised and perplexed. I can seek the favor of God anywhere I go and anytime I need." Jack had some clarity about how to approach God.

"Well said Jack! You know, I'm with you wherever you go." Faith held Jack's hand and they both walked out. Potter ran behind Jack and Faith.

"I will also follow you Jack." Potter smiled and looked at the church.

"Thank you!" Jack replied to Potter.

"Are you talking to me?" Faith asked Jack.

 Jack smiled looking at Faith.

***

Ruth was so serious and upset for what had happened with Jack in the Church. She sat in the couch and reading the

Holy Bible. Jack came out of his room with a backpack. She looked at him and kept the Bible on the stool. "Where are you going Jack?"

"Mother, I'm going to find my own way. Please don't follow me." Jack was so upset and disturbed and reluctant to stay in Pluckley village.

"You're leaving?!! Why?!! I want you to stay with me my son!" Ruth was so concerned about her son and didn't want to allow him to go away.

"If I stay in this village, I won't have a good future." Jack had decided.

"God helps poor people; he helps troubled people; if you trust God you will be fine wherever you are." Ruth realized and agreed to his decision.

"Okay, mother! I understand…I am only leaving you for a while. I will come back for you when I achieve something." Jack anticipated and looked at the coming future with hope.

"God bless you my son! I will be waiting for you right here." Ruth felt sad and afraid to stay alone, but she had no choice.

"Thank you mother, I'm sorry for leaving you alone for now…but I will never forget you for giving birth to me. Everything you've done to me…loving me and caring… Never…"

Jack became emotional. When she saw tears in Jack's eyes, she stood up; hugged him and soothed him.

***

Faith was sleeping in her bed. The door opened making a soft sound. Curtis entered; He approached Faith and slithered into the bed; he hugged her while she was asleep. He kissed her cheeks and exhibited sexual overtures.

Faith woke up suddenly and saw her step-dad. She got out of the bed quickly.

"What're you doing here?" She was angry and frustrated.

"I wasn't getting any good sleep. I thought you would need my company." Curtis was completely influenced by sexual intentions.

"I don't need your company. And I told you this many times." Faith warned him softly.

"Come on kid! We can have a good time together." Curtis was trying his best to tame her.

"You're sick…you know! I'm your step daughter! How could you think of having sex with me?" She raised her voice.

"I just see myself as a handsome male and you are a beautiful female." Curtis believes in a slogan 'the relationship between a male and female ends in a bed.'

"You're a sick pervert!" Faith wanted escape from that room quickly.

"Whatever! I want you baby!" Curtis was so rude.

Faith's mother coughed loudly from outside. Faith found a pistol from a table drawer and she pointed the pistol at Curtis.

"Please get out of my room; take care of your wife." Curtis got off the bed slowly with his hands up.

"Go easy on the pistol. I will leave…I will go!"

Curtis left the room slowly and fearfully looking at the pistol in Faith's hands. Faith howled aloud.

***

Jack was standing by the London expressway, and looking for lift. Faith approached Jack running fast with fear; she hugged Jack and said "Jack...take me with you, Curtis is coming to kill me". Jack nodded yes to her and looked around.

Curtis along with a couple of men was coming closer to Jack and Faith. Faith was breathing heavily holding Jack and laying her head on Jack's chest.

Curtis gripped Faith's hand very tightly and said rudely, "You…F****ing B***h!! How long has it been since you escaped from me?"

Faith was trying to release her hand and yelled, "Let go of my hand you bastard!"

Jack eased self and looked into the eyes of Curtis and said, "What's your problem Curtis?"

"You stay out of this...you loser. Otherwise!"

Curtis signaled his gang, and immediately they attacked Jack. Jack was so quick in his moves in defending himself.

The two strong men showed off their martial arts skills to beat Jack.

The highway is noisy with fast moving cars, trucks, and heavy vehicles. Jack observes their moves and located their weak spots. Jack attacked now and hit them hard and they fall onto the road. One man is hit by a car and his body flies off the road and fell on the road divider. He was in writhing agony and moaning. The second man fell onto the road, escaped being hit by a truck, and then ran to the other side of the road.

Jack spat on the floor. "Bloody Fighters…"

Curtis holds Faith tightly and points the barrel of his gun to her head. "Hold it right there Jack! If you come any closer I will blow her head off."

"Jack…you leave me here and go away." She pointed him towards her shoes.

Jack looked at her shoes. There he saw a pistol in her stocking. Jack lowered himself; showing his hands up. "Hold on…I just have to get my backpack and leave. You take her with you."

Curtis laughed cruelly, and licked the cheeks of Faith. "You see Jack. Your girl is mine and her mom is mine as well. You can take your bag and get the f**k out of here."

"Okay, okay. Don't harm her. I'm leaving." Jack bent down carefully, and moved to the bag that is placed next to Faith's legs. He picked up the pistol from Faith's stocking and shoot

Curtis in the leg. Curtis yelled and moved back and tried to shoot Jack, but Jack jumped and escaped the bullet. Faith moved back.

Curtis fell on the floor and moaned in pain holding his leg. Jack approached Curtis. "Please…don't shoot me." Curtis pleaded.

"You don't deserve to live you sexually perverted man!! Mark my words you f*****g punk." Jack pointed his pistol onwards the forehead of Curtis.

Curtis took some pills from his pocket and swallowed them, "I'm suffering from high blood pressure. Let me go!!…You can take Faith with you."

"Jack!! Don't leave him…he is a liar!! Kill him." Faith said aloud.

"When you decided you wanted to seduce and mentally harass your step-daughter you had no grasp of understanding that you would eventually become a dead man" Jack paused for a while and then looked at Faith and told her softly, "I can't kill a soul."

Jack still aimed the pistol at Curtis. Curtis wanted to escape; he looked around.

Then his personal demon approached him and whispered in his ear. "Curtis, cross the motorway. You will escape for sure."

Curtis quickly ran across the highway. While he was running, and trying to cross the expressway, a truck came very fast and hit Curtis. Curtis bled out and died.

Faith rushed to Jack and hugged him. She was afraid to see Curtis dying.

A gang of demons gathered around Curtis's body to celebrate his death. They were actually amusing themselves by seeing the bloodshed.

Meanwhile, Potter arrives there. "Hey Jack. How're y ou doing?"

"Hey Potter..." Jack whispered in Faith's ear..."Here is my invisible friend."

"What's happening here? I see a filthy gang of demons partying over that dead body." asked Porter.

"What are you seeing Potter?" Jack couldn't see those demons.

"The gang of demons - that cause accidents on the roadways." Potter explained.

"Demons…Accidents…" Jack was surprised and looked around. Faith also looked around in doubt.

"You know, there are many demons which are hanging around places like trees and motorways causing many accidents. Millions of them exist all around the world." Potter revealed the fact.

"I'm surprised to know that. Do you know why they do that?" Jack whispered to inform Faith about this. "Entertainment… ghost games…they see people bleeding and dying on the streets, motorways and some lonely places. They amuse themselves by seeing people's blood and deaths." Potter was sad to say these facts.

"Very interesting…I don't know about all of this." Jack blinks eyes and shook his head.

"Now you know. By the way, where are you heading?" Potter asked.

"We're moving to London to find jobs and settle there." Jack replied.

"London - that's a great place to find rich ghosts. Would you mind if I come to pay you a visit sometimes?" Potter requested.

"You're always welcome to visit us Potter." Jack held the shoulder of Faith.

"Thank you Jack much appreciated!" Potter whispered.

There came John running. "Hey…you two…where are you both going?"

"We're leaving for good." said Jack, but Faith was nervous seeing John.

"I thought you were leaving Jack. Only you…" John looked at Faith and approached her. "I told you I love you…many times! But you wanted Jack instead of me."

"I told you…I don't love you…many times! But you are after me constantly." Faith spoke boldly.

"I need you Faith…I can't leave you." John was pleading.

"Hold on John. She's my girl." Jack confirmed for the first time.

"She can't be yours. I spent a lot of money feeding her family, gave her many gifts from my childhood, and I also supported Curtis for a very long time." John recalled all the past.

"You gave me them John. I never asked for those gifts and I never accepted them." Faith wanted to clarify.

"Where is Curtis? I sent him here." John was looking around.

"He's gone a long way; you can't reach him now." Jack looked along the expressway.

"Well, enough is enough! Jack, you will fight me now. If you win you can take the girl." John wanted to go for a bet to win Faith.

"Faith is mine. I'm ready to die for her. Come on. Let's find out who wins." Jack was ready to fight.

"No Jack…he's going to trap you." Faith was afraid.

"I have faith in God and I trust you my Faith. Come on John." Jack was so confident and recalled a verse from the Holy Bible: 'Unless it is the Lord who protect the city, the guard on duty is pointless'

Jack and John began their fight for Faith. Potter looked keenly at them both.

"Hey…Guys…come and see this. There's another feast awaiting your presence."

Some demons approached Potter and stood behind him to watch the fight. They made some tribal sounds while Jack and John were fighting. Jack and John went on the motorway. The cars and trucks were traveling at maximum speed. They tried to escape from the cars and trucks to continue their fight.

All of a sudden, a truck hit John; his body flew off and falls on the other side of the road. All of the demons rushed to the body of John, enjoying seeing him bleed out and moan. John was going to die.

Jack looked at Faith at a glance. Suddenly, another car came fast and hit Jack.

***

Kick-Boxer Jack

Jack was on the hospital bed; he was wounded badly. Faith stood next to the bed and weeping.

A nurse was preparing some injection; a doctor entered and spoke with Faith.

"He needs some rest. We can stop the bleeding and he will be back to full strength in a week." Faith was bit relaxed and looked at doctor thankfully.

Frankie entered along with his secretary Rosy. Faith was looking at them and Jack was moaning with pain and he could not open his eyes.

"Doctor, what is his condition." Frankie enquired.

"He is gonna be alright in a week." Doctor replied.

"Thank you doctor, may I speak with him." Frankie asked.

"You may. But don't ask him any questions. Just tell him some good news." Doctor suggested.

"Understood doctor" Frankie assured and looked at Rose.

"Nurse, give him some antioxidant fluids." Doctor ordered nurse and left the room. "Okay doctor." replied nurse.

Frankie approached close to Jack's bed and looked at Faith and asked, "Friends?"

"We live together." Faith replied.

"Great. Jack, may I speak with you?" Frankie spoke softly.

Jack opened his eyes and spoke softly, "Hello…"

"I'm Frankie. I am the president of the National Sports Authority. I run the sports company and I make shoes and other types of sports products."

Jack tried to pull out his right hand for a hand shake, but he could not.

"No formalities. Your girl tells me that you're a gifted fighter…a tough guy huh." Frankie looked at Rosy and winked his eye. Rosy smiled.

"Yes, I do my best…" Jack replied.

"Okay…Good. Here is my offer. You want to work for me and my company? I will make a champion out of you." Frank spoke like a kind man, but a businessman too.

Jack looked at Faith, and she nodded her head. "Okay…I will fight for your company." Jack confirmed.

"Wise decision, I will make the arrangements for you both in London," Frankie looked at Faith, "My secretary Rosy will get you the rest you need."

"Thank you Mr. Frankie."

"My pleasure, it's hard to find talent like you in the city. Be positive and stay strong. Bye for now…See you both soon in my office."

"Alright Frankie, thanks!" said Faith.

Frankie left the room, but Rosy approached Faith and started speaking. Jack closed his eyes and moaned with pain.

Potter appeared there moved towards the bed to see Jack, and whispered.

"Hey Jack! Lucky escape! You know, there were some demons who tried to take your life. I managed to stop them though."

"Thank you Potter, I appreciate your help." Jack whispered.

"Anytime Jack! So…are you going to work for this guy?" Potter asked. Jack nodded yes and Potter looked at Rosy speaking softly with Faith.

"A hot chick…yeah…" Potter winked his eye. "You like her?" Jack smiled at Potter.

"Of course…Yes. She is hot!"

"I guess you might want to teach her about accounting and clarify some doubts she may have." Jack always found some fun and happiness talking to Potter.

"Once upon a time, I taught math and accounting. Now, I want to enjoy my life seeing different forms of beauty." Potter was happy and trying to engage Jack.

"But now…can you make that happen, Potter?" Jack expressed a doubt.

"I can see her anytime and anywhere I want to…you know." Potter stressed the word anywhere.

Jack smiled and said, "You are such a prick Potter."

Potter laughed a loud and said, "Yes, I am…I want to write my autobiography entitled "THE PRICK!" They both laughed this time.

***

London - Frankie's office... Frankie was on the phone sitting in his chair. Rosy came in and said, "Jack and Faith are here sir."

"Bring them in!" Frankie was reading some important documents.

"Yes boss." said Rosy. Rosy went out called them.

Jack and Faith entered Frankie's office while Rosy opens the door for them.

"Welcome Jack and Faith. How're you both? Are you both quite comfortable at our company's house? Please take your seats." Frankie looked at them keenly.

Jack and Faith sat in the chairs. "We are fine there and we thank you for your help." Jack said.

"It's a job offer my dear." Frankie was a perfect business man.

"Well…We're here to discuss that." Jack understood Frankie's point.

"Yes Jack. Here are the contract papers"

He opened his table drawer and took out a file and handed it to Jack.

"The terms and conditions are there. Please go through them. If you accept my offer, Rosy will take you both to our attorney."

Jack took the file. "Thank you Frankie!"

"Well, Rosy will lead you both to the waiting room. You two can discuss this and then report to Rosy."

While Jack and Faith along with Rosy went out, Frankie lit a cigar.

***

Faith and Jack were reading contract papers in the visitor's waiting room.

"Five years is too long." said Faith.

"We will sign for two years then." said Jack.

"Okay…I will inform Rosy about this." Faith went out in search of Rosy.

Meanwhile Jack was reading the contract document. Potter appeared.

"Hello Jack. How is everything going with you?" "Hey Potter. I'm going to work for Frankie."

"Good for you! FR Sports Company! Great establishment! I guess this guy Frankie has connections to politicians." Potter looked around.

"I'm not interested in politics and religions." Jack was just a fighter.

"I know…you're a fighter. A tough fighter indeed…" Potter acknowledged.

"You're right sir; it's in my blood." Jack stated.

"Blood…you know there are millions of blood thirsty demons out there spoiling people's lives; causing them to fight, face accidents, and commit suicides; bringing innocent souls down to misery." Potter revealed this information before.

Jack acknowledged and said, "I understand…there are some good ghosts out there like you, I guess."

"Well, I am an odd ghost; an outcast." Potter was looking around.

"Good for you Potter! I am glad I met you." Jack was happy.

"Well, I'm happy to see you alive. By the way, where is my Rosy?" Potter asked.

"She's with Faith, discussing our contract." said Jack.

"Contract? For how long?" Potter asked. "Two years." Jack replied.

"Let me go check out that beautiful woman Rosy. I also want to check out this guy Frankie. Let me see what is inside his mind."

"Well, I can't stop you Potter." They both laughed. Potter disappeared.

***

Potter appeared in the secretary's room. Rosy and Faith were discussing the contract. Potter moved close to Rosy and smelled her; felt good and looked at her from top to bottom.

"This woman is so intoxicating. But I can't stop it. Oh My God! She has a stunning body."

***

Frankie was speaking with a business partner on the phone in his office.

Potter appeared there; approached Frankie and turned around him and stood behind him; looked into his head; he could read his skull; surprised to see some chemical reactions in his brain.

"This guy's brain is full of greediness, lust, and filth."

Potter looked at his left hand and is surprised to see Frankie scratching his private part.

"Oh. This guy is scratching there. Dirty fellow…may be suffering from ringworm. Why don't you apply medicinal cream, man, that is disgusting and stinky…"

Rosy entered. Potter freeze and stared at her.

Frankie gave her some instructions regarding the contract of Jack and Faith.

"Let Faith be our model for promoting our products."

"Hey, are you stinky Frankie? You like Jack's girl Faith uh? You naughty, stinky Frankie..." Potter looked at Frankie's left hand resting in pants pockets.

Jack, Faith entered Frankie's office. Rose handed the contract file to Frankie.

Frankie read the contract seriously for a while and then counter singed on it. He stood up and handed the contract copies over to Jack and Faith.

"Welcome to the FR Sports Company Mr. Jack Reid and Ms. Faith Williams. I wish you both a pleasant stay and success with our company."

"Good for you Jack. All the best Faith (looks at Rosy). Happy days are approaching for us, my dear Rosy!" Potter whispered.

Rosy dropped a pen and bent down to pick it up. That was a visual feast for Potter. Jack and Faith checked their contracts. Frankie shook hands with both of them.

"I wish you all the best in your career with us!" said Frankie.

"Thank you Frankie" said Jack; "thank you Rosy" said Faith.

"Thank you Rosy! You are such a beauty! But your boss is stinky" Potter looked at him disgustingly.

Rosy felt someone was standing behind her. Jack and Faith left the room with Rosy. Immediately, Frankie's left hand began scratching his private part.

"Hold on Frankie! Let me leave too. Then you can scratch there the entire day." Potter said and disappeared.

***

The Lion of Babylon

AFTER FOUR MONTHS

FR SPORTS CLUB - DRESSING ROOM

Jack was wearing a tux; he moved in and out of the shadows. At 27, he was overweight, but was in perfect shape; his feet popped up and down like they were on canvas and his tiny fists still jerked forward with short bursts of light. He was rehearsing a nightclub monologue.

"Good evening ladies and gentlemen. It's a thrill to be standing here talking to all of you wonderful people. In fact, it's a thrill to be standing here right now! I haven't seen so many people since my last fight. After that fight, a reporter asked me, 'Jack, where do you go from here?' I said, 'To a hospital!' I fought twenty one professional fights and still none of them bums figured out how to defeat me -- they kept hitting me in the head! And that's why I'm here tonight"

Faith came in and they both started to sing. "Street Blood...I'm the Street Blood. I'm the best, don't try to test, you know the rest. I'm the wildest...in every contest."

Faith was singing chorus. "Street Fighter, street fighting man; you have to watch yourself while you're on the run!"

"How many times must I beat you? How many times must I support you? You just got pricked and you don't understand; you need to go home to be a family man!"

Chorusing by Faith… "Street Fighter… Street fighting man; you have to watch yourself while you're on the run!"

"I'm a predator and I wander in the twilight NIGHT! I'm a gladiator KILLIN' World Warriors who live for the fight! I'll beat you with my LEFT to end your poverty! I turn around and see myself a reformer of the poor! Street Blood… I'm the street blood. I'm the best, don't try to test, you know the rest. I'm the wildest…in EVERY contest."

***

FR SPORTS CLUB - NIGHT

Bam! JIMMY REEVES, a fast, black middleweight boxer jabbed JACK in the face. Jack staggered forward. No matter how hard Jack was hit, no matter how often, he always staggered forward like a bull.

The bell sounds.

Battered, Jack slumped on the stool in his corner. Faith and Frankie sat next to each other in the VIP box.

Audience -- each member screaming at the FIGHTERS in the ring.

Suddenly, words were exchanged. A GIRL screamed and a POLICEMAN and a CIVILIAN stood and started fighting each other.

And in the ring Jack took a swig of water and spat blood into the bucket while his helper JOEY holds for him; TONY his trainer works the cuts. "You didn't have to come to

LONDON to get beaten up by a "mighty hunter" Jack!" said Joey.

"He's got you Jack! You're outpointed! You're coming up for the tenth. You gotta knock him out!" Tony advised.

The bell sounded for the tenth round.

Jack pulled himself up and charged at REEVES. Reeves slide away, jabbing, punching, and piling up points.

In JACK's corner, Joey stood and yelled at Jack. "A grand apiece…We got a grand apiece on this Jack! A fucking grand…"

Jack suddenly cornered Reeves and unleashed a desperate, wild alley-fighting attack. One ferocious punch after another…The SPECTATORS gone wild; everyone stood up for the kill.

Reeves staggered and then fell onto the canvas.

The REFEREE counts: "One, two, three, and four..."

The GAMBLERS called out new odds - Ten to one for REEVES, the underdog.

Joey, excited, sees that time is running out and steps in front of the bell. He swung his arms, pretending not to realize he literally held back the TIMER's arm for a few seconds. This gave Jack more time for a knockout -- but not enough. Joey was pushed back and the bell rang at the count of nine, ending the match. Boos and cheers. The BETTORS scrambled back to the BOOKIE to get their money. Jack danced around the ring, kissing his gloves and thrusting them toward the CROWD.

Faith rushed out and hugged him.

A young man handed over a mike to Frankie. "Hello folks! Everything is fair at FR sports club. I congratulate Jack for his fighting skills. He made it to the finals and he's one step away from the championship."

While Jack and Faith waving their hands, the crowd yelled and clapped for Jack.

***

FR SPORTS CLUB QUARTERS - NIGHT

Jack and Faith were naked and going to make love.

Faith straddled him. Her hair was loose. It was cut straight across at the level of her shoulders. It was hanging forward, hiding her face, except for her eyes, which she was holding shut tight. She started kissing the lion tattoo on his face. Faith was taking her time.

The kiss, unbearably fragile, a spike of sensation, shoulders the frame. There were no words, only sensations, smooth sensations. Tender, like the tickling lick of a kitten. Faith felt powerless, suddenly stoned. Jack was kissing her. She was kissing Jack. They were standing in the middle of the bedroom, giving and getting every kiss they've ever gotten or given; kissing from memory.

Kissing: fast, hard, deep, frantic, long, and slow. They tasted the lips, the mouth, and the tongue. Faith put her hands to Jack's face; the softness of his skin; the absence of the rough scruff and scratch of a stale shave is so unfamiliar as to seem impossible. Jack rubbed his face against Faith's -- sweeping the cheek, the high, light bones muzzling the ear, the narrow line of the eyebrow, finishing with a butterfly flick of the lashes.

Faith was at her breasts. She was enjoying it. Jack was kissing Faith's abdomen, tonguing the caesarean scar that no one ever touches. Jack touched Faith's breasts, pressing. Her knees buckled, she collapsed to the floor. Jack went with her; carried her onto the bed.

"Pretty desperate aren't you?" Jack whispered. "Yes." Faith whispered back.

"For God's sake, why? We have plenty of time." Jack asked.

"How long?" Faith questioned.

"As long as you want..." Jack whispered.

She was dragging her hair across his eyes. Kiss me, he thought, anguished, because she wasn't going to, he knew. She lightly bit his shoulder. She was lowering herself more. She was brushing her breasts across his face. He wanted to take one of her breasts into his mouth, either one. He was frantic. He wanted to get as much of one of her breasts into his mouth as he could. He drove himself harder into her. She was whining with pleasure and that was good. She would climax again right away. He kept on going, slowing himself down. He pushed her knees up higher. He was almost there and so was she, again.

***

Jack and Faith were together taking a bath. Jack was standing behind her under the shower and was applying soap to her body. When his hands reached her stomach, he could sense something strange.

"What's the matter?" Jack asked.

"Your guess is right. I'm pregnant." Faith confirmed.

Jack tried to lift her up in happiness, but stopped. He thought because of the soap, he might slip her.

"I'm so happy for us, and for the baby." Jack looked at her admiringly.

"A baby boy." the eyes of Faith were so bright. "Is it a Boy?" Jack's happiness was doubled.

"Yes, I came to know it yesterday." Faith reconfirmed.

Jack turned her body and embraced her. The water showered all over them.

***

NATIONAL SPORTS AUTHORITY AUDITORIUM

The Announcer entered the ring with a microphone. "Attention please! Attention! Ladies and gentlemen, tonight we have had the rare privilege to have witnessed the greatest exhibitions of stamina and guts ever in the history of sports."

The Crowd roared.

"Now for the evening's main event -- In the corner of my right, the Challenger, wearing white trunks -- At one hundred and ninety-one pounds, one of Frankie's best fighters -- "The Babylonian Lion," Jack Reid!"

As soon as the announcer mentioned the name of Jack, the crowd yelled in response.

"In the far corner, wearing red, white, and blue -- Weighing in at two hundred and ten pounds undefeated in forty-six fights -- the Heavyweight Champion of the World -- "The Master of Disaster" -- Antonio Breed!"

Sooner the announcer finished, the Referee motioned to both fighters. They stepped to the center of the ring. As the Referee explained the rules, Antonio and Jack stared hard into each other's eyes. The Referee's voice faded away and the fighters' communicated something soulful and frightening expressions.

"Now fight." When the referee shouted, the fighters returned to their corners.

Frankie approached Jack at the corner and said "This is going to be a tough fight Jack."

"Thanks Frankie -- I'm will do my best." Jack looked at Frankie.

Faith was not seen there. Jack looked for her and Frankie understood that.

"She's at the hospital" Frankie took a slip out from his pocket, and handed it to Jack.

Jack read "For our baby. Love, Faith." Jack felt great and folded the paper slip and then put it in his mouth.

When the bell rang, Breed danced forward and boxed Jack as though he considers the man an amateur. The arena exploded and Breed put on a display of hand speed.

Commentator #1 said, "The Champ stings the slower challenger with jabs at will -- Reid blocks eighty per cent of the blows to his face -- Breed doesn't look the best he's ever been but is moving smoothly -- Breed snaps out a triple combination that backs Reid into a corner -- oh, a solid hook by Breed, a master of fists- men."

Commentator #2 continued, "The Champion is smiling and toying with the man -- trying to give the fans their money's worth and make a show of it with the badly out-classed challenger -- Another left to right combination. I feel sorry for --"

Commentator #2 was interrupted by Commentator #1.

"Breed is down!"

Jack suddenly exploded with an upswing hook to the jaw. Breed was dropped. The arena exploded. Breed's eyes show disbelief. So did Jack's. Jack backed into his corner.

Frankie came to the corner and said, "You can do it! Goddamn it, you got the power! The body, get the body!!! You got him going!"

Referee began counting. "Six!…Seven!…Eight!…" Breed was up…His playful attitude was gone…

He was now all business. His lightning jabs stung Jack's face repeatedly.

Breed yelled. "Come at me sucker!"

Jack charged and a terrific right hook crashed against Breed's chin, followed by an uppercut to the liver that causes Breed to cringe. Breed countered with jabs and Jack whipped brutal combinations to Breed's body.

The bell rang.

JACK'S CORNER

Jack asked Frankie. "How'm I doing?" "Really good!" Frankie answered.

"Do you see how fast he is? Damn!" Jack was impressed by Breed's skill.

"Breathe deep -- Keep your chin down!! Use your legs and drive through him. Attack – Attack… Attack…" Frankie cheered.

BREED'S CORNER

Breed did not sit. He stood and clowned around with the spectators to prove he was not hurt.

Breed spoke with his trainer, "Damn. That boy almost broke my arm."

"Sure -- He can hit -- Don't play no more -- Stick an' move, hear?" Trainer advised.

"I'll carry him 'till the third." Breed told the trainer.

"Don't play with this man, he's fighting hard -- Let them feel some real heat!" The trainer replied.

 The bell for the second round rang... Jack rushed out fast and furious. Breed melted out a left hook that raised a goose egg over Jack's eye, and he employed footwork that dazzled Jack. He had class. He studied Jack and employed his lightning jab with cutting accuracy. Still, Jack shuffled ahead, bombarding Breed's midsection with his hooks.

The round ended with Breed assaulting Jack with blinding combinations and delivering a stupendous right cross that flings Jack into the ropes and shattered his nose.

The round ended. Breed stood in his corner. Though he was joking with the fans, he was beginning to show the strain from Jack's body punches. "Man, I rearranged his face with that right cross. The people love what's happening tonight!" Breed spoke with his trainer.

"Everyone is not concerned about your pride right now!! Breed, you are in a fight my man -- you better best believe what you hear. Knock that boy out soon so we can all go home." Trainer warned.

Jack sat at the corner. Frankie and Rosy were trying to reduce the swelling around his eyes. His nose was shattered.

"Your nose is broken." said Frankie. "Damn! How's it look?" Jack questioned.

"Can't tell... Don't swallow the blood -- Go for his ribs. Don't let him breathe." Frankie answered.

"This guy's great." Jack looked at Breed.

"Why don't you tell him you're a fan?!" Frankie advised.

The Commentators got caught up in the action. They spoke rapidly into their microphones.

Commentator #2 said, "If you had asked anyone who knows boxing, they never would've predicted a first round knockdown and the second round with punishment to the body of the Champion. Most fighters will tell you that receiving a good body punch is the next worst thing to dying."

Commentator #1 announced, "Round three is ready to start and should be interesting to see if Breed can put the challenger away"

There goes the bell. Round three began.

Breed came out dancing. He skipped and side-steps to dodge Jack's sledgehammer hooked. An expert ring general Breed used the ring fully. Jack kept tearing in and Breed met the bombing attack that caused thick swelling. Near the end of the round Jack fired a penetrating punch to the heart.

Commentator #2 said, "Breed almost sprints out of his corner -- feints and throws a pair of left-right combinations. Jack drops beneath a left uppercut and lands a very solid shot on Breed's temple -- not much movement from Jack, duck a left, a right, another left, and explodes with a right hook to the temple -- I mean he explodes with a right hook. The Champ backs off."

Commentator #1 continued, "There's no way Breed expected this kind of hitting power."

Commentator #2 agreed to his partner, "No way -- but the brilliant ability of the Champion to master situations like this is one of his most outstanding traits -- Breed tosses a perfect right hand that rocks Jack backwards. Breed is now playing offense -- Reid takes the heat and counters with a left punch to the heart. Whoa!! That must have hurt!!"

The wallop knocked Antonio off balance…Jack released a terrifying uppercut that opens a gash under Breed's eye. Breed's face contorts with excruciation.

Breed's trainer began yelling, "Cover your face! Cover up!" and he looked at his assistant. "My man's cut, my man's bleeding -- Get ready!"

The Bell rang.

Breed's corner worked frantically to close the wound…The ring doctor inspected the cut.

Breed's trainer asked the doctor, "Bad? Talk to me man!"

"Deep…but passable..." Doctor replied.

Staring at Jack, Breed said, "That man's taking his job too seriously."

"He's moving to your left -- don't let him move there anymore -- dance and stick, hear? Don't play. I know what you feeling, but don't play." The trainer instructed Breed.

"He got lucky." Breed told the trainer.

"Luck! You fighting a crazy man -- but you hurt him bad." Trainer looked at his assistant, "More ice, now!"

JACK'S CORNER.

Jack's face was in very bad shape, not cut, but wretchedly swollen around his eyes.

"How you holding up kid?" Frankie asked Jack.

"Fine...but I'm fighting with the world champion. That guy's great." Jack looked at Breed.

"Give me the water! You are getting tagged by his right. I think you should feint left and high hook him" Frankie looked at Breed and said, "Rosy, check his eyes! Can you see?"

Jack stood up and asked Frankie, "See what?"

"You're draining him of his strength -- He's losing steam."

"He isn't losing anything!" Jack felt Breed was so strong.

"Keep on him -- You're doing great." Frankie cheered.

In the next ten rounds, Breed cut and slashed Jack to ribbons, but pays dearly...Both his eyes and lips were cut.

***

N.S.A AUDITORIUM CAR PARKING AREA - NIGHT - The same time Jack was fighting with Breed.

Faith was sitting in her car; breathing heavily and panting. She looked like she had drugs and fully intoxicated. She was almost out of control, but she was holding her belly and crying.

***

N.S.A. AUDITORIUM - NIGHT

The championship fight continued…The men were fighting with appalling tenacity. Jack ripped into

Breed's body…Breed countered with a ceaseless stream of rapier-like lefts…The Challenger is seriously outclassed, and said, "C'mon – Let me cut you!"

Jack waded in and Breed employed incredible footwork. He set himself and cut loose with a thunderbolt right cross to Jack's chin. Red droplets were already dripping from his broken nose… Blood sprays from the wound. Now Jack was facing merciless beating and is staggered by a torrent of combinations. Jack's eyes were closed. But Breed cannot drop him.

The Bell rang!

The Commentators shift in their seats.

Commentator #1 said, "Without a doubt this is the most punishing brawl the audience and I have ever seen -- with blood. This fight should have been stopped rounds ago but Jack Reid refuses to fall."

Commentator #2 continued, "Not only has he refused to fall, but he has beaten the Champion's body without mercy and the bout has become a vicious slugfest.

Breed's corner is in turmoil…The Champion was definitely hurt.

"My side..." Breed looked at his trainer. Trainer ordered his assistant, "Get that doctor." "No doctor!" Breed yelled at his trainer.

"You're hurting man!" The trainer warned Breed. "No doctor…I'm feeling good bro!" Breed denied.

In Jack's corner, things were frantic. His eyes were swollen shut.

"Want to keep going?" Frankie asked. "Would you keep going?" Jack asked Frankie. "…Yeah." Frankie answered.

The bell rang.

Breed moved cautiously out of his corner and circled to Jack's right. The Commentators stared at the fighters without an answer.

Commentator #1 began saying, "The fight has slowed down to a near standstill -- Breed circles to Jack's right… The spectrum is nearly silent -- Neither fighter has made a motion to throw a punch…I've never seen anything like it in the last round of a championship fight…"

Breed spat blood on the canvas. It appeared he is protecting his right side. His ribs were probably injured at the end of round fourteen. It's confirmed, unofficially, Breed's ribs may be broken -- Breed Antonio fakes a left and throws a big tired right -- Jack Reid's mouthpiece was out! Breed attacked with one hand!

"Breed might have lost his hand" Commentator #2 announced.

Breed feinted and Jack fell for it. The Champion unleashed a lethal blow to the side of the head that jolts Jack's mouthpiece into the second row…Jack sagged against the ropes in a crucified position…The insane crowd leaped to their feet.

Jack's bloody teeth snarled at Breed and he waved for him to come ahead and fight toe to toe. Breed obliged with a weary but effective burst of rights and lefts that have K.O. written on every punch. Jack countered the assault blow for blow.

"Give me your best!" Jack totally became insane. Frankie looked at the clock.

TEN SECONDS TO GO.

"Give me your best!" Jack said again.

Blood sprayed over the ropes and onto the ringside photographers... They were horrified and wiped away the blood. The fighters stood toe to toe and dragged every remaining bit of strength from their souls and bet each other without mercy. They look hypnotized and have entered a dimension far beyond blood and pain.

SIX! FIVE!! FOUR!!! THREE!!!! TWO!!!!! ONE!!!!!!

The BELL RANG…The arena EXPLODEDS with thunderous approval.

The corner men rushed to their collapsed fighters. In the midst of the entire confusion, both fighters looked at each other with unabashed respect -- They stood like blood-drenched gladiators on the most dramatic night of their lives. As though reacting to some unspoken command, they both step towards each other and embrace.

Breed Antonio whispered in Jack's ear. "…any chance for a rematch."

"I don't want one." Jack replied.

Frankie came over and separates them and led him back to his corner. Frankie embraced Jack.

The Announcer enters the ring with a microphone. "Attention, please!! Attention!! Ladies and gentlemen, tonight we have had the rare privilege to have witnessed the greatest exhibitions of stamina and guts ever in the history of combat sports."

The CROWD ROARED. The announcer continued, "Judge Walker scores it seven-seven Breed. Judge Samuel scores it eight-seven Jack.

Breed was rigid. Fear radiated from his eyes. To lose the crown on this night after the fight he fought would kill him. A silence has blanketed the arena and waited for the final result. The announcer broke the silence, and aside, "Both the judges score it nine-six Jack…Winner and Heavyweight Champion of the World, Jack Reid!!"

Frankie and Jack looked at each other and grinned. Frankie hugs Jack like a son. Frankie raises Jack's hand again. Jack turns away from Frankie and stares across the ring at Antonio Breed, who stands desperate, and his face and body are badly distorted.

Jack climbs out of the ring and the fans crush forward screaming his name and waving red, white and blue banners. Frankie's eyes show mounting apprehension as the fans become abnormally active.

Jack's and Antonio's fans are aggressively competing against each other chanting, 'Jack, Jack, Jack.'

Jack is completely at the mercy of the crowd. He is being passed overhead and remains helpless as his body floats up the aisle on the sea of hands. The Chanting is deafening.

***

Jack lost Faith!

FR HOSPITAL – The Same night; Jack, Frankie, and Rosy rushed to the hospital and reached the operation room. They were tensed. Doctor came out.

"What happened? How is she?" Jack asked.

"I'm very sorry Jack. She's no more!" Doctor declared. Listening to the doctor's statement, Jack collapsed.

"How did this happened doctor?" Frankie asked.

"Faith died of an overdose on drugs. She underwent tremendous amounts of stress which led her to consume very harmful drugs." Doctor explained.

Rosy approached Jack and tried to soothe him.

"This is all very unfortunate doctors" Frankie approached Jack. "I'm sorry Jack! This's a great loss for you and for the FR Sports Company."

Jack could not believe that Faith is gone! He cried aloud; his cry resounded in the hospital.

***

EAST LONDON BURIAL GROUNDS – NEXT DAY
FAITH'S FUNERAL

Faith's mother Mrs. Williams, Jack, Frankie, Rosy and other staff members of the FR Sports Company gathered at the burial grounds. Majority of them were wearing black clothing.

Faith's mother was speechless, moaning constantly. She was so sick and Jack held her while she walked.

Frankie led the procession, containing the coffin and the funeral flowers - white lilies. This ritual was called 'paging away.' The pager, Frankie walked a short distance before getting into the hearse.

Friends and colleagues stopped and paid their respects.

The priest prayed and thanked the family, friends, and relatives of Faith for all of the favors which were done for her.

Jack handed over Faith's mother to Rosy and rushed to the coffin. He paid homage to Faith with white lilies and he kissed the body of Faith, touches her womb, and kissed her stomach before she was covered with the lid of the coffin.

"Let us commend Faith Williams to the mercy of God, our maker and redeemer." Priest stated. The coffin is lowered into the grave. Jack cried aloud. Priest continues, "We therefore commit her body to the ground; earth to earth, ashes to ashes, dust to dust; in the sure and certain hope of the Resurrection to eternal life."

The staff covered the grave with earth. Frankie ordered his men to place the gravestone.

The Assistant Priest read from the Book of Revelation. "And I heard a voice from heaven saying, 'write this: Blessed are the dead who die in the Lord from now on. Blessed indeed,' says the Spirit, 'that they may rest from their labors, for their deeds follow them.'"

Main Priest closed his eyes and began to pray, "Father in Heaven, I thank you for your child Faith. Father, this is such a bittersweet time for us all. Faith's faith was so evident in how she lived her life. She was the type of woman that would lay her life down for any one of her friends and family members. And Father, she has a lot of friends. We all love and miss her dearly, but we know that she is in a much better place now, walking down the streets of Heaven and with Jesus. Lord, we are thankful for our friend and we anticipate seeing her again in Glory. May Your Name be praised always! We love and thank you for our beloved Faith. Amen."

Jack kneeled down at the grave.

Frankie approached him and said, "I'm deeply sorry for your loss Jack."

Jack was silent; he was looking aimlessly at the grave.

The priest approached Jack; laid his right hand on Jack's head. "The Lord is near to the broken hearted, and saves the crushed in spirit." It is written in Psalm 34:18, Father in heaven, look at this man who has lost everything and is now sitting here. Please forgive him for his mistakes and grant him peace in his life. In Jesus's holy name I pray, Amen.

***

JACK'S QUARTERS – NIGHT

Jack was sitting alone in the living room drinking whisky.

Mrs. Williams was in the bedroom weeping for her daughter and coughing frequently.

Potter appeared. "Good evening Jack. I'm sorry for your loss."

Jack didn't answer. Potter sat across from Jack in a chair. Jack cried aloud and said, "How can I live without her?"

"I know Jack…you loved her very much. And she loved you more than her life." Potter acknowledged.

"She was carrying our son... I lost two people at the same time." Jack voice was breaking.

"Oh… My God!" Potter was shocked.

"God has shown no mercy on me!" Jack was angry with God.

"All of a sudden…What happened?" Potter asked.

"She consumed a high dosage of drugs and died of cardiac arrest." Jack couldn't control his agony.

"I see…I guess something is not right. At one time…she's happy and pregnant. How could she just die all of a sudden?"

"I can't believe this Potter…I have no clue and I have already lost My Faith." Jack began thinking.

"You stay strong Jack. I will probe around and get you the facts about the mystery of her death."

Potter stood up.

"Thank you, my friend…I'm waiting right here!" Jack was in grief and angry the same time.

"Take Mrs. Williams to the best hospital; show her to the specialist doctors. She has been suffering for a long time." Potter advised.

"I will…Thank you" said Jack.

"See you soon, Jack" Potter disappeared. Jack moaned and couldn't control his pain.

***

PLUCKLEY VILLAGE - DAY

Jack arrived driving his own car. He waved to some people who are standing by the road and near some shops. Most of them were surprised to see him and happy for his accomplishments.

Jack drove to Mrs. William's house. Mrs. Williams came out of the car. She looked healthy. Some neighbors were surprised to see her active and in a sound body.

Jack and Mrs. Williams entered her home. "Mother, may I see her room?" asked Jack.

"Yes my dear! Go ahead and find out what she has kept for you." Mrs. Williams pointed to Faith's room.

"Thank you mother" Jack went inside Faith's bedroom.

Jack was curious and searching for Faith's belongings. He found a picture of himself in Faith's cupboard drawer; he grabbed it and then put it in his pocket. Also, he found a note on her mirror quoted "You can give without love, but you can't LOVE without giving."

"You loved me a lot Faith; you gave me everything you had. I can't believe you are no more!

Come back my love, if possible! How can I live without you? Jack kneeled down and wept…

Mrs. Williams entered and hugged him and wiped his tears.

"I know Jack…you both loved each other very much. Faith was so kind and she couldn't heart an insect; she used to stop me from killing cockroaches in the kitchen." Mrs. Williams couldn't stop her agony; she wept. "She told me one day that 'You have no right to take a life."

"She has been inside of my mind the entire time; I can't bare this pain mother."

Jack cried aloud while she tried to soothe him.

***

JACK'S HOUSE – THE SAME DAY

Ruth was sitting in the couch and knitting a sweater.

Jack entered. Ruth got up, welcomes him; and kissed him on his temple.

"Long time, mother, how are you?" Jack embraced her.

"By the grace of God, I'm good." Ruth replied.

"Did you receive the money?" Jack enquired.

"Yes my dear. Thank you for sending money every month." Ruth was happy.

"My son is a Champion now…I'm happy…But…"

"What happened mother?" Jack asked.

"As long as you feel it is right hurting people in the boxing ring, I am upset for your profession and I won't approve of your ways of life." Ruth told how she feels about his job.

"It's just a sport mother." Jack explained.

"But…these blood sports hurt people, in some cases animals. People are watching those fights and competitions for pleasure and they are betting money on their favorite competitors. What's going on Jack?" Ruth revealed her thoughts about blood sporting activities.

"Well…it's my job to do this; I can master some more fighting skills and I only know how to knock-down my opponents." Jack was defending.

"Okay…Good for you Jack. I'm not satisfied with your achievements and your success." Ruth sounded rude, but she had her intuitions.

"I lost my Faith, especially my faith in God. I don't know how I'm going to survive without her." Jack busted and knelt down at her feet.

"Chosen people will come to Jesus! Somehow, God brings them refined and prepared for the cosmic battle." Ruth wanted reveal the will of God about chosen people.

"Very well mother…I wish I were you. Let me go and find my own way of life for now." Jack stood up and ready to leave.

"God bless you, my son, perhaps you might want to see Pastor Joseph before leaving." Ruth suggested.

"No thank you mother! Not today…God bless you too!" Jack left sadly.

Jack went to Pluckley Village Lake before leaving his village. He sat by the lake where Faith used wait for him. He felt sad sitting alone and he recalled memories of Faith. Mary Jones came there by bicycle; she approached Jack. Jack turned back and was surprised to see her.

"What a pleasant surprise…" Jack couldn't believe she came for him.

"How're you Jack?" Mary asked.

"Just surviving…" Jack answered with broken heart and breaking voice.

"I heard about Faith, I felt depressed."

"I lost all of my hope…" Jack looked into the lake waters.

"Ask God. He will give you peace." Mary suggested. "I will…Thank you Mary."

"Are you staying or returning to London." Mary enquired.

"I wanted to stay. But I signed a contract with the FR Company. So I need to return." Jack didn't want to go back.

"Okay Jack…you're a champion; remember this village needs you; you are the inspiration for the youth." Mary encouraged him.

"I won't forget my native place Mary… I'll come back." Jack assured.

"Thank you Jack" Mary shook hands with Jack.

"You're welcome Mary… thanks for coming." Jack was pleased.

"Bye Jack! I need to go now." Mary left.

"Bye Mary!" Jack felt someone behind.

Potter appeared. "Welcome my friend!" Jack didn't expect him there.

"Hey Jack...how's everything?" Potter was happy to see those woods and lake.

"You know how I'm feeling." Jack replied.

"Yes, I know. I saw Mary speaking with you; she's a nice person; what do you say?" Potter looked at the way Mary returned.

"I really don't know Potter." Jack was reluctant to talk about any other woman.

"Okay…never mind; are you going back to London?" Potter asked.

"Yes…" Jack confirmed.

"May I go with you?" Potter asked. "Why not…" Jack said.

"Thanks buddy. Let's go!" Potter jumped into the car.

***

Jack was driving back to London.

Potter was sitting with him in the front seat. "Watch your driving Jack…I heard something brushing up against your car." Potter sensed something.

"What's that?" Jack asked.

"A group of demons are talking about you and they want to play tonight on this motorway." Potter explained.

"Well…I'm not afraid." Jack said.

"But I'm afraid. Honestly, I don't want to die again." Potter was chuckling.

"Are you kidding me?" Jack asked.

"Yes…I am just joking. But watch your pedals please." Potter whispered.

"Okay sir. I will." Jack changed the gear and drove the car.

Potter was looking around and suddenly saw Clara asking for a lift, showing her thumb, which was burning. Potter waved at her. She recognized Potter and smiled. Potter motioned his hand for her to get into the car. She jumped into the back seat of the car.

"We have an unseen guest in our car Jack." Potter said.

"Who's that?" Jack asked.

"Madam Clara, the principal with a principle." Potter always wanted to amuse Jack with his humor.

Jack couldn't see or hear Clara, but Potter can see and speak with both Clara and Jack.

"How's everything going with you Potter?" Clara asked.

"My life is so…so dreadful Ms. Clara." Potter answered.

"I heard someone from the Village died." Clara was asking about Faith.

"Yes, Faith, his fiancée, died lately." Potter clarified. "His girlfriend…?" Clara asked.

"Yes Madam Clara! Do you know anything about her death?" Potter enquired.

"You mean the young lady who died in the FR compound…?" Potter got shocked.

"Yes, indeed! She was working in the FR, as a brand ambassador." When Jack heard Potter, he asked him, "What are you and Clara talking about Potter?"

"I'm trying to gather some information about Faith's death." Potter said.

"What have you got Potter?" Jack was exited.

"Hold on, I'm extracting some information about this case." Potter whispered.

"Oh! My Potter, her death was horrible!" Clara saw her death.

"What did you see? Could you please tell me?" Potter moved to the back seat.

"My boyfriend liked boxing and he went to see the kick-boxing championship tournament." Clara was revealing Faith's death secret.

"Did you see how she died?" Potter sat humbly next Clara and asked.

"Potter, is there any clue?" Jack couldn't wait.

"Please hold on Jack. I will tell you what Clara tells me… everything" Potter whispered.

"I saw that lady running towards the auditorium…Faith was late and was running to see the final match. She was running in the corridor. Her sneakers' laces were loosely winded up and the hung laces stopped her. She bent to tie up her laces and there was a blast sound. She heard it come from underground. She was curious and kept her ear on the floor to hear the sound clearly. She realized that there is something happening in the basement. She looked around and found a secret passage to the vault. I followed her. She was surprised to see what's happening in the basement. Frankie's men were making illegal drugs on one side and illegal arms on the other side. She was trying to come up, silently, but Frankie's brother Ryan found her. He put his gun to her neck and said, 'You shouldn't have come here Faith.'

"Who're you...how do you know me?" Faith asked in fear.

" Of course...I know you are FR's brand model." Ryan answered.

"I see...FR is involved in illegal business." Faith asked him boldly.

"FR is a monarch in this country; we do whatever we can to support our political systems." Ryan spoke proudly and fearlessly.

"But it's not the right thing to do." Faith forced her hand to move the Ryan's pistol from her.

Ryan signaled for his men to seize her. Two men come forward and detained Faith tightly.

Ryan tried to call Frankie but could not get him online.

He messaged to Frankie about the situation. There comes the reply on the mobile screen.

'KILL'"

Potter was telling the story to Jack.

"Ryan looked at a drug maker. "Doctor X, could you please give her a massive dose?"

"Okay boss..." Doctor replied and prepared an injection and approached Faith. Seeing him come towards her, Faith tried to escape and screamed. Ryan looked at Doctor X.

"Please don't kill me. I'm carrying a baby." Faith pleaded.

"It's SR's orders. I can't do anything." Ryan declared. Doctor X injected dangerous liquid into her shoulder. Faith, felt dizzy…but gained strength…pulled self from the strong hands of Ryan's men and ran towards the exit. Ryan quietly sat near the CC camera monitors.

"Don't go after her. Let her go…she's gonna die in two minutes." Ryan told his goons.

Faith ran up of the basement and reached the main door of the auditorium. She saw Jack fighting…and she shouted aloud, "Jack…Jack…"

A couple of bouncers stopped Faith from entering inside and they pushed her out and closed the door. Faith fell on the floor; she had almost collapsed and could not control herself.

After a few seconds, she opened her eyes, pulled herself up, and ran toward the car parking area. She opened her car and boarded it. She sensed something…she was terribly panicked to see a lot of blood came out of her vagina.

"Oh! God…help me…" Faith cried for help.

Jack stopped his car suddenly and cried; yelled aloud. "Faith…My love…" Jack cried like a small kid.

"Please control yourself Jack." Potter tried and sooth Jack.

"Potter, ask him to calm down and guide him to take revenge. I have some work in the vicinity… I'm out of here. Bye." Clara disappeared.

***

Potter and Jack reached London and went inside Jack's Apartment.

"Dear Jack, before we discuss Faith, I want to tell you a secret." Potter said.

"What is it Potter?" Jack asked.

"My name is Potter, Potter Reid; I'm your grandfather." Potter removed the mask he had been wearing all the time.

"My eyes are really blue…" Jack leaned to the wall in the living room.

"Yes, my dear…Jack…My grandson…" Potter tried to embrace Jack in vain.

"That doesn't make any difference; I'm in great loss…"

"I know Jack. I apologize for not revealing my face to you all these days" Potter didn't want to reveal all the truth about their lives and family to Jack. The time came now…

"Tell me what I need to do now?" Jack asked.

"Stay calm about Frankie; relax and don't reveal your emotions." Potter had a plan.

"Then…" Jack didn't get his point.

"First, ask him to cancel the contract between you and the FR." Potter advised.

"If he denies…" Jack questioned.

"Request him to do it…Tell him that you're broke without Faith.

Also tell him you can't fight." Potter wanted to save Jack from Frankie.

"Sounds good to me... Then what…" Jack asked.

"We need time to estimate Frankie's strengths and weaknesses; then we will have to hit the nail on the head." Potter revealed his plan.

"Okay Grandpa…Thank you for being with me on this journey." Jack wanted to kill Frankie, but convinced with the plan of Potter.

"Anything for you my dear…" Potter felt warm.

"By the way…how had you been with women, when you were alive?" Jack asked.

"What do you mean?" Potter couldn't get Jack.

"Any problems with the opposite sex…" Jack wanted to know the past.

"I just had one beautiful girl…a poor girl from a village…I loved her very much and I wanted to marry her…" Potter was sad.

"And you couldn't marry her because she was poor?" Jack asked.

"I'm sorry my dear grandson…" Potter felt guilty.

"Four generations. You know, four generations have had to suffer for your mistake…" Jack has had some intuitions.

"Four generations…" Potter was perplexed.

"A man's mistakes…over the course of four generations will be punished…" Jack was referring to the Bible verses.

"Four generations…I count three only." Potter was mentioning Jack, his dad and himself.

"Four generations; it was you, my dad, me and my son…" Jack collapsed and cried.

Potter got shocked to know the truth.

***

Unavoidable Revenge!

Frankie and Jack were having coffee sitting on the couch in Frankie's office.

"I'm sorry for your loss Jack. She was like a nightingale here at FR." Frankie said.

"Yes…she is all in my mind…she's my love and destiny." Jack sipped coffee.

"Yes, I agree. Are you feeling any better now?" Frankie asked.

"Not yet!" Jack answered.

"Life goes on Jack; sometimes we need to go with what we have never expected." Frankie wanted to keep Jack fighting for his company.

"With all due respect, I can't do that Frankie." Jack spoke boldly.

"What do you mean?" Frankie asked.

"I request you to cancel the contact between us; and please let me go back to my village." Jack requested.

"Seriously…? That's not a wise decision. Faith's gone… you may get one more girl, and continue your life with FR." Frankie suggested.

"My Faith is gone and I lost faith in myself. Please let me have a break…"

Frankie got up and goes to the window.

"Do you by any chance, want to investigate her death?" Frankie asked.

"Investigate?" Jack questioned.

"I mean, do you have any doubts about her death?" Frankie questioned.

"I wonder why she took an overdose of drugs..." Jack expressed his doubt.

"Frustrations...maybe...I will ask my men to find out what exactly happened..." Frankie approached Jack. He wanted to console Jack and hide his crime.

"Thank you Frankie. You're so kind." Jack was underplaying.

"Anytime Jack." Frankie shook hands with Jack.

"Let me know about the contract." Jack reminded.

"Well...We will discuss this tomorrow." Frankie smiled.

***

That night, Jack was looking at the place where Faith was found dead in a car at the FR Auditorium car parking area.

He lit a cigarette, inhaled heavily...and looked around. He looked down at the floor...He could see some marks...He looked at the marks very keenly and closely... Those were marks of legs...Marks of walking legs? No...Marks of dragging legs...Somebody dragged her into a car...

***

Next day morning, Jack was getting ready to go to Frankie's office. When he was wearing his shoes, the doorbell rang. Jack approached the door and opened it. Frankie was standing there. "Good morning Frankie." Jack wished.

"Very good morning Jack, May I…" Frankie wished and asked for permission.

"Yes, please come in" Jack replied and Frankie entered.

"Just wanted to pay you a visit…Where're you heading to…" Frankie asked.

"To your office…" Jack replied.

"Well…great! I thought about your request" Frankie came with a plan.

"Please give me a break, Frankie…" Jack requested.

"I will give you a break; I will release you from the contract…"

"What do I need to do for that?" Jack s ensed Frankie's plan.

"One more championship fight…It's my request; our FR shoes sales are no good.

I want to have another competition to promote sales for our shoes." Frankie wanted kill Jack.

"What are you talking about Frankie? FR sports shoes are great and comfortable." Jack doubted and couldn't believe Frankie.

"But we are competing with world- class shoemakers Jack; we need to boost our sales for them…" Frankie had valid point.

"Okay, I'm with you." Jack said confidently.

"Thank you Jack... Just one more tournament…and one last fight…I will release you from all the trouble…" Frankie senses someone is behind him. Yes, Potter was behind him, waving to Jack.

"Yes Frankie…One last fight…for you and for FR" Jack agreed happily and smiled at Potter. Frankie left.

***

Jack was taking a shower that night. Under the water, it sailed like silver down the contours of his face and neck. He was in that zone of concentration where the best athletes undergone…where the premotor cortex activity dominated and facial expression became blank. His eyes looked distantly…Jack's in his domain…in the groove.

He recalled his bath with Faith. Also, he recalled their promises: When Faith asked him, "What would you do if I die?" "I can't live without you my love" Jack promised her. "Remember…do not kill any person or animal intentionally" Faith ordered him. "I won't kill" Jack promised her.

Jack cried…and cried…remembering Faith, and his tears mixed with water.

***

FR Auditorium was ready for the next tournament. Jack was almost ready for the fight waiting in the dressing room. Rosy was assisting Jack, wrapping his hands, ripped the tape into narrow strips to go between the fingers.

Potter observed the wrapping. In addition to its function, the taping felt ritualistic.

Jack's attention was focused elsewhere…on his action: what he will do, his strategy.

Trainer Jo called from the doorway, "Countdown… Countdown!"

"The countdown is on Jack. Five minutes." Rosy said.

Jack got off the training table. Rosy had finished. He put on his robe, checks himself out in front of the mirror, tossed some punches, and did a quick warm up for a full minute.

Jack and Potter went to an alcove. Potter blessed Jack.

"Four minutes!" Trainer Jo shouted.

Rosy was putting sealed bottles filled with honey, orange juice, and water into the water bucket. As Jack put on the robe, the others gathered up the gear and then start out. Trainer Jo moved to Jack preparing for his entrance, to be as close to him for the cameras as possible.

"Give us a moment. Alone…" Jack looked at Jo, and said "Hey. This is my religion!"

Jo and the bodyguard followed the others away from Jack. Rosy began applying Vaseline on Jack's face. They were alone in the room.

"It's hot and humid…Monsoon season is about to start. It might hit 120 degrees in the ring under the lights. Are you alright Jack?" Rosy asked.

"I'm fine?" Jack looked up and said, "Ryan isn't any harm to me. He's knocked out eight out of eleven of them before the end of the third round. He is the most dangerous fighter I have ever fought."

"I'd worry if I was hearing anything else." Rosy said and finished applying Vaseline. Jack loosened up his neck. "And I can't wait!"

"Three minutes!" Jo shouted from outside.

"Dance…That's the most important thing to do for this fight…" Jack looked at Dundee enigmatically. Before Rosy can ask…

"Forget about every battle of man against man, of mind against mind, of soul against soul. This is the one. This is the greatest." Rosy whispered. Jack nodded to her.

"This is it." Rosy whispered again.

"Two minutes!" Jo shouted from outside.

"The prophet's not who you think he is! Get the pretender off of that throne!" Rosy spoke philosophically.

"Rumble young man, rumble! It's the 'Rumble in the Jungle!'" Potter said aloud.

Jack's camp started moving towards the door. They opened the door. It is guarded by a handpicked squad of paratroopers.

"One minute!" Jo shouted.

***

Paratroopers were on either side like a wedge, guarding Jack, Jo, Rosy, as they pushed their way through the door and out into the hall. As they travelled with Jack, people at the end of the corridor saw Jack.

The chant began…"Jack, Lion of Babylon! Jack, Lion of Babylon!"

The sound from the corridor picked up a second reverberation that booms from a distant vast space. As Jack and his crew moved toward it to encounter it they suddenly…Burst out into the stadium...

***

Lights flooded FR Sports Auditorium. They poured down artificial sunshine onto the ring.

"Jack, Lion of Babylon! Jack, Lion of Babylon!" Roars ascend from a thousand voices at a quarter of four in the morning. The moon is out, revealing storm clouds.

Seeing Jack and the entourage, the crowd went on nuts, travelling with Jack with the mass, the crowd kept roaring, Jo behind, Rosy on one side, Potter invisible, and other attendants.

***

Jack entered the ring. They cheered. Jack raised his hand and saluted them. Jack danced from one end of the ring to the other…danced into Ryan's corner…The crowd roared.

Jack danced back to his corner…

"Ryan is playing prima donna. He wants to make you wait." Rosy guessed.

Jack laughed. You won't psyche out Jack with that stuff. Instead, Jack used the time. He tested the ropes. He got a feel for the distance between the center and the corner. He circled the ring. He looked at the crowd from different angles, from the corner, the center…He looked up at the lights and adapted to the heat from them.

Jack's feet did a shuffle. He felt the canvas underneath his feet. He felt the soft spots and the firm spots. He felt how much slide there is because of the resin on the canvas, how much spring there is in the boards…

Jack shed his robe and then threw a blistering array of jabs and hooks. The crowd went nuts. Jack looked into the ringside and saw…

Suddenly, Ryan came in from the extra arena isle. He came out in his red robe with his men and cheer girls. Frankie entered the auditorium and reached his VIP seat.

"Ryan! Ryan! Ryan! Ryan!" Crowd yelled.

Jack was shadow boxing in the ring as Ryan climbs into the ring and walked near him. The look on Jack's face was indifferent. Ryan went immediately to his stool. He didn't move around the ring. He didn't touch the ropes.

The referee moved to the center of the ring. A great roar filled the air: "JACK, JACK, JACK! LION OF BABYLON!" … another one. "RYAN! RYAN!"

As Jack, Ryan, and both of their crews met in the center of the ring Referee Clayton made an announcement. "Now, both of you know the rules. When I step back, I want a good, clean break. No hitting below the belt, no kidney punches, no…"

"Clayton, you're about to discover you are nothing." Jack said.

"Jack, be quiet!" Clayton warned.

Ryan's eyes glared. Jack rocked back and forth, ready to rumble.

"No kidney punches. Now fight…" Clayton finished his instructions. Jack past the referee eyeballed

Ryan, and said "You've been hearing about me for years. All your life you've been hearing about Jack Reid. Now you gotta face me."

"Jack, I'll disqualify you if you don't stop. Now, I want a good, clean, sportsmanlike fight…"

Clayton warned, and said, "Now go to your corners and start fighting when you hear the bell. And may the best man win."

Jack turned his back and continued to shuffle and shadowbox.

Jack and Ryan's corners were clear. Jack was facing his corner, praying to God. Ryan was looking at his brother Frankie who is bent over at the waist, flexing and releasing the remaining tension in his huge shoulders, as the bell for ROUND ONE clangs…

Both charged in the ring and stopped as if they ran into a brick wall five feet from each other. Then Jack dipped, threw a left, which Ryan took on the shoulder...a BIG RIGHT HAND to Ryan's head.

The crowd went mad. Ryan clinched, picked up Jack, and swung him 180 degrees through the air with his power. As he put Jack down, Jack pushed Ryan's head down and away and Jack clocked him with ANOTHER RIGHT. Ryan clinched and drove Jack back to the rope.

Jack threw ANOTHER RIGHT that landed. Jack danced, circled, and stayed out of Ryan's way. Then he slammed him again with a right.

Ryan lured Jack into a corner and threw vicious combinations and a hook that nailed Jack in the body. And a wild shot hit Jack on the side of the head.

Jack was stunned as he just taken a damaging shot from Ryan. He pushed Ryan, the stronger man, out of the way and danced and circled around him. Ryan tied him up again. Jack pushed out, danced and hit HIM with a RIGHT. Jack tied him up, and there's the BELL.

Jack was talking to himself at his corner, "Legs heavy…air's heavy…like sand…"

"Slowly move in on Jack" as Rosy and Jo's talk fades away. Jack's awareness in a deep concentration is amazing. He was holding counsel with himself. Jack stared into the space across the diagonal to the other corner, but not really at Ryan. Jack was weighing something. A gamble...He blinked, and whatever it is, he's decided it NOW. AMBIENT SOUND started to come back as Jack's attention returned to the present and he ignored this.

"Keep moving. Don't let him trap you in a corner. Stay off the rope!" Jo advised.

The bell for round two rang.

Jack charged into the center of the ring, provoking Ryan to chase him, and Jack immediately backed into the rope and stayed there, seizing opportunity, Ryan threw big hooks. Jack was doing exactly what he's not supposed to do. He got off the rope and backed into the rope on the other side. Most of the shots were blocked by the gloves of both men. No damage. Then Ryan threw a left which Jack blocked and then a big right hook. Jack turned away. Nevertheless, it crashed into his jaw.

Time slowed down. Jack tied up Ryan. Jack was injured. Dazed...But he must make Ryan believe he's uninjured.

"That all you got...? That's it?" Jack teased Ryan.

Ryan reacted. Jack took vicious hooks to the midsection, hanged on and moved right back onto the ropes, tied Ryan up.

Ryan's shots were taken on Jack's elbows and gloves. But for every four that are thrown, one or two tremendous hooks got through to the sides of Jack's ribs.

Jack's face revealed impact, but nothing diminished the TERRIBLE FORTITUDE with which he endured. Now, he tied up Ryan. But then Ryan drove Jack into a corner and pummeled him.

Rosy and Jo were going crazy in the corner.

"Get off the ropes! Get off the ropes! Get off the ropes! Dance!" rose yelled.

Jack was blocking and getting hit. There were worried faces in the crowd who supported Jack. One woman looked away. Jack's eyes were alive and are more than alert, the sharpest eyes in boxing.

Ryan's left jab came in. Jack feinted and shifted. It missed Jack by a quarter of an inch. Ryan hooked off his jab. Jack leaned back on the top rope.

Ryan's punch fell short and connected with little effect. That's how good Jack was. The techniques became clear. Ryan went upstairs and threw three hooks. They all got taken on Jack's gloves. Ryan slammed a hook that began in Cape Town and ends up in Zaire, into Jack's abdomen. And another... Jack took the shots and hanged on.

Jack's eyes were bright like stars. His white mouth guard shined. A grimace…A grin…

"There is nothing…Nothing." Jack was speaking to self. Another one of Ryan's hooks landed…"I cannot take this anymore." Jack pushed Ryan off and connected with a left and a straight right to the jaw. They pound but didn't stop Ryan. Jack tied him up. Jack's jabs ended the round. Nothing effective, but Jack shook his head disapprovingly, put his hand on the back of Ryan's neck, and as the BELL sounds…

"Thought you were bad" Jack whispered. Ryan laughed. He won the round overwhelmingly.

Jack's corner was apoplectic.

Here came Ryan's "murder" round, which referred to Round Three.

Jack pushed away from his handlers and rose. He opened his arms to the crowd. Massive crowd yelled, "JACK, LION OF BABYLON"

Jack opened his arms as if the roar of a thousand voices is sunlight. By opening his arms, his skin soaked it in and converted it to power. And the BELL STARTS ROUND THREE.

They traded. Nothing happened. Ryan advanced. Jack backed to the ropes and tug Ryan with a couple of harmless left jabs. Now Ryan opened up with heavy artillery. Jack got in a couple of shots, but for the center of the round he was pummeled by Ryan. Midway through the round, Ryan accepted a left jab and while Jack's left arm was out with it Ryan hammered a right cross into the exposed lower midsection of Jack and then followed it with six tremendous hooks to Jack's abdomen. Jack pushed him away.

Ryan came in again. Ryan got him on the rope again, and a surprising right on the left side of Jack's face. Jack tied up Ryan's left in the crook of his elbow, and they staggered, married, awkwardly, into the center of the ring. The referee separated them.

Ryan was charging and throwing heavy shots. Jack took some on his elbows, arms, biceps and shoulders. NOW, Jack leaned back. WAY BACK. 45 degrees back…there was the TWANG of the rope. Jack was using the rope as a shock absorber. Some of Ryan's punches got through, but the rope TWANGS and Ryan was hitting a trampoline with a hammer. Between deflection and being ring-wise, Jack diluted much of what Ryan throws. Then Ryan drove three powerful hooks into Jack's side. Jack's body spammed but as if it was inconsequential.

"Ryan! Show me something." Jack challenged. Jack was insulting, taunting, snapped jabs into Ryan's face, talking through his mouthpiece…

"Where's your punch man?" Jack teased Ryan.

"Jack, get off the ropes! Stick them! Jab! Off the ropes…" Jo shouted.

Jack blocked a rage of Ryan's headshots with his fists and the abdominal shots within his elbows. Each one of Ryan's punches was a haymaker. RYAN suddenly switched from the floor: Ryan's uppercut slammed right through Jack's guard, right into his jaw. Jack got hurt, but he didn't lose his grip.

"Off the ropes…Dance, champ, dance…" Rosy was yelling.

Jack pushed back self like a rag doll. Ryan threw a right hand. It too slammed through Jack's guard. He's in trouble.

Jack's eyes flashed, rolled in his head. He saw neon.

Time slows and lights dimmed…

"Been here before..." Jack slows down and babbled. He could vaguely hear Jo's voice, "Jack, move! Dance champ!" Jack glanced at the crowd.

Ryan slammed shots into Jack's kidneys and ribs. Jack will piss blood for two months. But Jack stayed on the ropes. As time catch up to normal…Jack thought that he was losing, but he spoke with Ryan, "That's all you got? That the hardest you can hit?"

Jack came off the ropes, and hit Ryan with a terrific three-shot combination; a right-left-right. WHAM- WHAM- WHAM. Jack Feinted and hit Ryan with another left-right. WHAM-WHAM.

"Come on chump!!!" Jack roared.

The Bell rang.

It was a Jack rally at the end. He threw Ryan a look of contempt as he walked over to his corner.

"Get off the goddamn ropes!!" Jo yelled.

"Took something away from him... Jo that round…" Jack replied.

"You gotta move! Stick and MOVE!" whispered Jo.

Jack told to himself, "They don't know what's happening."

Jack looked to the left and sees Frankie, and said aloud, "You bet the wrong horse! He can't fight no better than you can act!"

Frankie laughed.

The Bell rang. Round Four

Jack is braced on the ropes, as far back as the ropes will go. Ryan threw a barrage of shots; he slams in five and six at a time. THE BELL RANG. Jack protected himself with his gloves at his head. Elbows at his ribs. When headshots came in, Jack slips to the right or left, or turns them into glancing shots, or just leans straight back so that they all fall short by a quarter of an inch. The BELL RANG. Jack covers himself, taking the most powerful hooks Foreman has thrown in the fight, one after the other to the body.

Jack was speaking to self, "Take it! Terrify him with what you can take…God, I'm losing strength. If you want to spare my life, please give me strength"

Jack's eyes were stars. He saw everything. He saw things no one else can see in the quantum physics of deflecting the force of Ryan's blows.

Ryan was desperate. He pounded a left to Jack's side, a blocked left to the head, three lefts to the belly, which get through. Jack's left arm convulsed downwards, involuntarily, with the blows. What Jack's not ready for and didn't block was the right hand that follows. This shot was jarring and concussive. He grabbed Foreman's neck and had to hold on.

The BELL RANG.

IT WAS MID-ROUND SEVEN

Leaning way back at impossible angles, Jack was soaking up Ryan's shots. Ryan was SLOWER…BUT Jack was not throwing at all!

Ryan hissed to Jack, "Eight more rounds…You running outta gas?"

Then…Jack smirked and came out from under. WHAM. WHAM. WHAM. WHAM. WHAM. Five hard shots were followed into Ryan's puffed face. They surprised and enraged him.

Ryan drove Jack with his 220 pounds…Ryan's arms and fists now SWUNG HEAVILY. Some got through. Jack's right eye was puffy. Both tied up. And then THE BELL ended the round.

JACK'S CORNER

Rosy and Jo were talking softly. Jack couldn't hear them.

Jack began speaking to himself and Ryan. "Can't let you get that second wind which you don't know is out there for you (talking to Ryan in his head). Want the title…wear the heavyweight crown (to himself)? Jaw broke? Nose smashed?

Face busted? You ready to die? Is this you (towards Ryan)? Cause you gonna meet a man who will die before he lets you win."

Potter walked by…As he passed near Jack, he had the audacity to wink at him. Jack happened to saw it. He winked back at him. He smiled. He brightened right up.

THE BELL RANG.

Jack went to the ropes, threw a couple and, now, came off the ropes. He was in the center of the ring. HE WAS HUNTING. A couple of lefts from Jack, Ryan threw a haymaker and almost fell out of the ring. Jack was in the corner, having avoided the shot. Ryan got in a couple of lefts that Jack deflected. Jack took another on the cheek, leaned way back again. Suddenly, he seemed tired, as is Ryan. Tied up, they went diagonally to the other corner of the ring, both fighters exhausted, leaning against each other. Resting... BUT…

Jack's eyes were dead sharp. He was faking. Ryan backed Jack into the corner. Jack hit Ryan with a left. Ryan launched a short left that Jack countered with a BIG RIGHT CROSS that connected. Ryan's head snapped around. Sweat sprayed in a parabola of light. The crowd ROARED with expectation. Ryan tried a right uppercut, failed as Jack circled, guiding Ryan onto the ropes. Ryan was on the ropes then.

Jack's eyes knew the moment is…he spoke self "Now…"

Jack's short, chopping right turned Ryan's head down. Ryan came over the ropes and turned back into the ring…JACK'S

RIGHT HOOK slammed his head down and sideways. And RYAN charged back into JACK.

Jack snapped a combination: an overhead right to Ryan's face, a short chopping left, and a right hook. Jack's eyes lit up like white phosphorus.

Jack continued to speak self, "RIGHT NOW!"

Ryan wrestled Jack into the center. And the most significant moments began...

Jack's left hand was extended way behind him with his wrist bent, no power. As it passed his body, Jack converted it into a left hook. As he's doing this, he's dropping his left foot back. His left foot didn't support his left hand. It's for his right hand so the body can untorqued across with the punch. And Jack was already cocking his right. Meanwhile, the left connected with Ryan's jaw and raised his chin. As the left was departing Ryan's chin, Jack launched his RIGHT.

As Jack's right hand came in, Jack's torso untorqued, transitioning all 217 pounds to Jack's left foot and putting that weight and power behind his right fist that crashed into Ryan's chin...and the impact transferred to Ryan's skull...and Ryan's head snapped around. He was gone. He was falling in a spiral…a metaphor for vertigo…turning downward into unconsciousness. And through the spiral, Jack had moved with him, pivoting with the falling Ryan, his right fist cocked to unload again if he had to. He never did…

Frankie is furious…he couldn't believe that Ryan was defeated and almost dead.

Ryan was down. Jack was pushed into the corner by Referee Clayton. Ryan was counted out. Clayton raised Jack's hand. People went crazy! TOTAL CHAOS… Jack was seized by Jo and other people around him.

As Jack was finally released from the suspense, the sky opened outside. The monsoon began; he closed his eyes and saw the face of Faith was the smiling.

***

Ryan's dead body was placed on a table in the hall of Frankie's palace.

Frankie was enraged and boiling with vengeance; seeing his brother's dead body. Jack and invisible

Potter entered the hall.

Jack approached Frankie closer. Frankie yelled "Jack… Jack…"

Jack smirked at Frankie and said, "Thank you…for asking me to fight the last fight for you. I won…For you and for the FR Company."

"You won…but I lost my brother." Frankie bit his teeth with soreness and vengeance.

"I didn't know he was your brother…I know…Ryan killed my Faith." Jack revealed the fact and surprised Frankie.

Frankie got frustrated and asked, "How do you know about this?"

"I know all of the secrets about you and your illegal business." Jack looked into the eyes of Frankie.

Potter came close to Jack and whispered, "Let me go and check around Jack!"

Jack nodded yes.

"I'm surprised Jack! Now, you will have no right to live. I'm gonna kill you here and keep your dead body next to my brother!" Frankie yelled and moved back; removed his jacket and shirt; expanded his body muscles…getting ready to fight.

Jack was warming up and getting ready to fight as well. Rosy was looking frustrated in a corner; holding a water bottle. Frankie's goons were ready attack Jack, waiting for Frankie's order. Frankie signaled to one of his goons.

A strong man of Frankie's attacked Jack. Jack punched him hardly. The man of Frankie was frozen in shock. His face became pale, the blood drained from his mouth. The other two men attacked Jack. Jack was so high in his fighting spirit, used his martial arts skills to pin down those men. A quiet whimper escapes from Frankie's lips as he looks down. All his men were just a bloody mess of mangled meat. A real horror show... Frankie staggered backward, shrieking. His hands were shaking. Staring down at the awful wounds of his men, Frankie thought of attacking Jack, in disguise!

The Hall is full of statues around. Statues of sun god, moon goddess, and other pagan gods were standing near the walls and in those statues, there were some demons hiding. Frankie was hiding behind those statues, one after the other, playing with Jack.

Jack, however, was prepared both mentally and physically. He blocked, avoided, rolled, jumped and redirected the attacks on him, making his way across.

Jack is about halfway across when an especially fierce a nd large statue comes crashing towards him. The demon inside was yelling, "Die…Jack… die…"

Jack caught a little off guard but he quickly adjusted and managed to spin out of the way.

Suddenly, as he turned and tried to catch his breath, two huge, deadly spears were streaking towards him. Jack blocked the SPEARS with his arms, misdirecting them into the wall behind him. They THWOCK into the wall, sticking there.

As Jack rounded a particularly difficult series of statues, a volley of ARROWS came HURTLING towards him. Jack blocked some, avoided others, and caught one in each hand. He threw them down and continues on. He went past the few remaining statues and was out of the Chamber. All that is left was to walk down a little hallway and out the door.

Jack looked behind him, and then he started to walk. He went cautiously, expecting a trap or a trick. Nothing happened. He got to the door and looked for a handle on the door. He spotted a handle near the top of the door and pulled on it with his hand. Immediately, his hands were locked in and a panel in the ceiling dropped right onto his arm, forcing it down. Jack fought back with his muscles, the veins popped out of his arms and neck. Behind him, a statue was started coming towards him, spinning like a dervish. Its fists and legs were extended, and they were deadly.

Frankie appeared and lunged for Jack's throat - Where Jack broke Frankie's grasp in a violent struggle - then punched him. Blood flew from Frankie's mouth. He frantically tried to break free for the surface - But Jack pulled him back down, and held him down, pushing down on Frankie's shoulders. Frankie was thrashing about, flailing in all directions, pounding at Jack…Then Frankie fell still.

Jack yelled and said, "Come on…kill me Frankie, I don't want to live, I want to go to my Faith, my love is waiting for me."

Jack was bleeding a lot of blood. A demon approached Jack, and whispered, "Come on kid…that's the spirit…die and go to live with your lover." Jack laughed a loud and freaked out.

Potter was standing next to Rosy, and worried about Jack. He began yelling while Frankie was pounding Jack, "Jack…kill that bastard…you need not die in the hands of this wicked person…you need to live for Faith, and kill for her."

Jack hit the wall and collapsed. He almost lost consciousness, bleeding to death…gasped and closed his eyes; and began speaking with a breaking voice, "I can't live without my Faith...I can't kill a soul...I promised her."

Potter closed his eyes and praying, "God...it's not fair... please do not leave Jack's hand...he doesn't deserve a pathetic death...please help him."

Frankie took out a sword from the wall and flew to Jack. Blink. Suddenly, when Frankie was about kill Jack with his sword, a terrible head-ache attacked Frankie. Everyone in the hall shocked and couldn't believe what happened. Immediately, Potter approached Jack, "Get up Jack, take that sword and kill him."

Jack couldn't open his eyes, but he was laughing and speaking softly, "God, take my life...I don't want to live...I don't want to live..."

Frankie felt thousands of swords were pinned in his head; he moaned... and moaned constantly. Rosy rushed to Frankie, "Boss...what happened to you" She was shaking Frankie's body, "Boss...what the hell happened to you?" She looked at Jack who was panting, smiling and dreaming of Faith.

Frankie felt a knife piercing deep into a nerve cluster in his neck; Frankie whimpered aloud, and paralyzed. Rosy couldn't that terrible pain in the face of Frankie; she closed her eyes.

Potter approached Frankie and said, "I know you...Murderer of innocent people. You're going to spend the eternity of your life drowning in a lake of fire...for the things that you've done. Did you know that?"

Rosy approaches opened her eyes; held Jack and tried to feed water to Jack from a water bottle that she was carrying; Jack was not aware of it as he couldn't open his eyes; When Rosy was about to pour water in the mouth of Jack, Potter rushes to Jack and whispered, "No…my son…there's poison in the water."

Jack opened his eyes and threw the bottle on the floor. Rosy ran away fearfully.

Frankie was shuddering and suffering from terrible headache. He looked at his brother's dead body, and spat out blood and water. Some demons surrounded Frankie, enjoyed to see him suffering; celebrating death.

 Jack gained his strength, opened his eyes and said, "You know, Frankie, I want to kill you so bad. However, I can barely contain myself. But I keep thinking that death is far too merciful a fate for you."

Frankie was hit by a stroke -- struggling to free self from the pain, felt as his head catches fire… a fate somewhat worse than prison. All the demons in the room few out yelling, "A good man dies or a bad man dies – all is a sporting feast for us!"

***

Jack was driving back home from London to Pluckley Village. Potter is sitting next to him.

"Son. How're you feeling now?" "I'm happy grandpa!" Jack replied.

"Is there anything still haunting you?" Potter asked. "Nothing…" Jack replied.

"Are you sure?" "Nothing…Wait a second…"

"Is there something bothering you in particular? Potter intervened.

"Yes, the dream; I always see a white horse, smoke, and two men." Jack recalled.

"That one man is your dad and the other man is the one who killed your dad." Potter explained.

"Who's the other man, who killed my dad?" Jack asked eagerly.

"You saw him Jack; and he died while you were watching." Potter unfolded the truth.

"Who's that?" Jack got surprised listening to Potter.

"Curtis - the step-dad of Faith…He killed your dad twenty-five years ago." Potter revealed the secret.

"Curtis…was he?" Jack was perplexed first, and realized what had happened.

"The plans of God are amazing!" Potter smiled.

***

Jack and Mary were speaking with the local and national press and TV reporters in the church campus.

News reporters with both the movie and still cameras were ready to record what Jack had to say. "Thank you all for coming to witness our church youth meetings. I am happy today and wanted to share many things about my life; the chosen people will come to Christ and they are chosen to co-work with God; I lived a pathetic life; terribly afflicted by my past; sins of my ancestors' haunted me; but God of mercy gave me deliverance; I, from today, live my life with honesty and integrity. I wanted to educate people about the bloodthirsty games, such as gladiator fights, bull- fights, and any other games that hurt animals and people; they should not be encouraged and they should not be shown to the innocent people by entertainment people."

The reporters started asking questions.

***

Potter and Clara are sitting on graves behind the church.

"Thank you Clara for helping me!" Potter said. "You're welcome sir!" Clara replied.

"Well, I need to finish up a lot of work, would you be willing to help me?" Potter requested. "Of course Potter, let's do something good!" Clara shook hands with Potter and immediately they disappeared.

Are there any good demons? No. There are some good spirits.

***